I'll B

By Eileen Charbonneau

Print ISBN 978-1-77362-202-6

A quality publisher of genre fiction.
Airdrie Alberta

Dedication

For my mother, another Kitty

Chapter 1

January, 1942
Port Washington, Long Island, New York

The closet was scented with furs, old oak, a riot of perfumes. And him, impatient, in the dark.

His fingers traced her stocking's seam. He reached higher, higher. *There.* He gasped when he encountered no obstacles. She'd left her panties on the dressing table. Kitty wanted that always — to be able to surprise him.

His finger slid inside her cleft. Was he gauging her reaction to his mad choice correctly? He needn't have checked. Kitty had been wet since he'd rolled the pocket door closed.

Circles now, knowing the arc of her desire so well he covered her mouth with his to quash her cry.

"Now?" he asked.

"Yes."

She felt him — smooth, hard. It was another exotic sensation, heightening all the others. He held her bottom secure so that, even standing — yes, one foot, then the other slipped

5

out of her shoes, circling his back as he thrust harder, deeper.

He blasphemed softly as he came, and then hid his forehead against her neck. She loved even his very Catholic shame, which he applied to his duty to satisfy her, not just broken commandments.

"Forgive me. I am a beast."

"Nuts to that," she proclaimed, slicking back his curls. "We did just right, flyboy."

He laughed. "Yes? Then you must do away with culottes forever."

He eased out of her. Kitty let the folds of her silk slip and the blue velvet gown drift over her legs again. She heard the orchestra begin a lively Peabody. Dessert was over, dancing begun.

"Philippe. They'll be looking for us."

"Who? Not your boorish husband?"

She laughed softly as she commandeered his crisply starched handkerchief to wipe her lipstick smears from his mouth and neck. "My husband?"

"He is not armed tonight, I hope."

She grinned. "To the teeth."

"There are better things to do with teeth."

He dove toward her ear, his mouth making a smooth landing, as they were almost the same height.

The orchestra began another tune.

"My husband—" she tried again.

"Is a fool, an imbecile," he claimed, buttoning his trousers with quiet efficiency, "for ever letting you out of his sight."

"I keep telling him that."

"Shall I try?"

She laughed. "He's not dim, but he is dense! And you might have to speak French."

"As it happens, my French is excellent."

Footsteps sounded, coming closer.

"Jeepers!" Kitty dropped to her knees. "Where's my shoe? Philippe! Help me find my other—"

They were granted only a slight warning cough before the narrow shaft of light widened and the closet's pocket door disappeared into the wall with a well-oiled click.

Jack Spencer, handsome in that toned, effortless way of the very rich, shook his head. Standing beside him, a sapphire-laden woman sighed elaborately as she tapped Philippe's shoulder.

"Really, Captain," she said. "*Plaisir d'amour* with one's own wife? Such narrow taste is hardly Free French, is it?"

A sly grin took over Philippe's mouth. "But I am not Free French but a Quebecois, a Canadian, remember? And now, a new American, thanks to my wife, Madame."

"Well." She turned her long-lashed disdain upon Kitty. "Small wonder with all that influence."

Jack Spencer stepped into the skirmish. "Some compassion for our newlyweds," he said as he stooped, then presented Kitty's red velvet shoe with a courtly bow.

"Yours, Cinderella?" he asked, his voice as dry as his favorite Vermouth.

She really was Cinderella, Kitty thought. She'd been on the receiving end of Jack's kindness since she was a line girl at his perfume factory. Her fairy godfather had provided much more than a promotion to Spencer International's switchboard. The new position brought Philippe and his mad, quick courtship into her life, and now, even after they'd made their vows at St. Michael's, his crazy lovemaking.

As Jack slipped Kitty's shoe on, Lady Emily Kenwood straightened Philippe's collar, making that simple gesture look scandalous in the process. And to think I was only nervous about using the wrong damned fork in this joint, Kitty thought, as Jack retrieved the Englishwoman's fur coat and tried to lead her to the door.

But she turned to tap Philippe's cheek.

"Do help us win the war soon, Captain. Save me from this tedious exile so we might meet again in London. Or Paris. And have a good flight, my darling."

His grin evaporated. "Madame," he said, with a curt nod.

As Jack squired Emily Kenwood toward the entry door, Philippe led Kitty through the gothic windowed hallways and back through the Palm Court with its orchids blooming in the dead of winter. She was breathless by the time they rejoined the festivities in the ballroom, where a soft, crooning version of *All of Me* began. Philippe held her close, his mouth soft against her cheek, like when they danced at the Savoy Ballroom uptown. But Kitty was not distracted by his grace or nearness, or by the candlelit room and its elegant guests, even when she recognized Broadway stars, two Roosevelts and an Astor among them.

"Why am I the last to know?" she whispered.

He breathed into her hair. "Ah, Emily only desires it to be true that I was once one of her conquests. In Paris we—"

"About the flight, Philippe," she redirected him.

"The flight," he repeated. "After the party," he said, spinning her out, than back into his arms. "I planned to tell you then."

Kitty felt her jaw tighten. "You were going to resign your commission in the RAF when America got into the war, too."

"After this assignment, Kitty. Then I will teach others the work, only."

"The assignment that strangers know about before I do?"

"I did not say she is a stranger."

He was trying to pull her into a fight about an old flame. Kitty knew he was no choirboy before their marriage. This must be an intelligence mission, or he wouldn't stoop so low.

The band's soft notes grew intimate. "Would my Kitty forgive me, if I find her some silk, perhaps a beautiful—"

"I'm not a child, Philippe. You can't sidetrack me with presents."

"Of course. I only wish to see you smile, and not worry about me. I want to carry that picture of you in my heart. It is selfish of me, I know. *Merde*. It was selfish of me to ever begin with you."

"Don't say that. Please don't say that."

"Forgive me. I can do nothing in the right way tonight. Listen. We must get out of here. Jack will loan us a car. Come with me."

"Where?"

"Not far. To the airstrip. Perhaps my thoughts will come together better there. They have to. Kitty, tomorrow I leave."

"Tomorrow?" she repeated.

He pulled her closer for the last notes of the dance.

"Tonight is ours," he whispered at her ear. "It does not belong to Jack Spencer, or the service. Here, now, under this moon, it is ours."

* * *

Luke Kayenta often marveled at how Turquoise Mountain gleamed under the light of a full moon. But this astonishing sight from the aeroplane's window was different. The city of New York was lit, not by the moon's reflected light, but by shimmering jewels, each beaming from within. Too many to count, like the stars. How could he describe his vision of the shining city to his mother and grandmother and sisters, in a way that they would not think him witched?

"I see it!" Nantai called to him.

"What do you see?"

"The building. The one the great monster climbed."

Luke sighed. Was he going to be berated again, for their off-duty night during training, the night he went into town to go dancing and missed the showing of King Kong at the base? No. He was not going to be berated, or teased. His clan brother's face was serious.

"I see the great needle tower, Adits'ah — from here in the sky!"

At the sound of his sacred name, Adits'ah, He Understands, Luke's attention focused. Only his family knew the name, and used it carefully.

"It is called The Empire State Building," Luke remembered from the guidebook his mother had ordered for them at Babbit's trading post.

"The monster fought the aeroplanes from that building," Nantai declared. "We should go there, some day. You could find it, you track well, for a college boy. It was a great battle, my brother! She cried out, the woman held in the monster's fist. She was not beautiful, like our women, but she split the clouds to honor her grief."

"So you told me," Luke said deliberately, trying to slow down his clan brother's uncharacteristic rapid-fire, scattered speech.

It did not.

"We could slay the monster King Kong. Like Changing Woman's twins."

"Maybe we could."

"The *belegaana* think we can help them restore the world, like our own monster slayers did. That is how I see it."

"Maybe that is the path we're on."

"But you don't know?"

"No, Ashkii Dighin," Luke addressed his clan brother by his sacred name, Holy Boy. "For that we have to trust Mr. Spencer, and," he tried to keep from wincing, "the government of the United States." Trusting the government of the United States went against almost every part of his being.

"There is no ceremony for this," Nantai said.

"Ceremony?"

"For us going through Skyland, this place that belongs to the stars. Like the journey Eagle Boy took. We are in a forbidden place, brought here by the ones who have been our enemies, and we have no ceremony for it."

He spoke with the wonder Luke shared, but Nantai's voice was also edged with terror.

That was it, then, Nantai was trusting him with his own fear, treating Luke like a medicine person..

"Sa'ah naaghai bik'eh hozho," Luke urged his clan brother quietly as the plane descended. Find your balance. Walk in beauty. The complicated philosophy of what it was to be a Navajo embedded in a few words. He wondered what else to say to give Nantai peace. Remember. Remember who you are.

The craft found its lighted airstrip and landed with a force much stronger than any truck or even the fastest train he'd been on. Luke had to swallow spit to clear his ears after the descent. Finally, all was still.

Nantai hadn't moved.

Two uniformed men strolled down the aisle. One pounded Luke's shoulder.

"Well, chiefs, what did you think of your first flight?"

His clan brother's shoulder pressed against his. "I will lose face with these people. I can't stop shaking," Nantai whispered in the Dinè language.

The men walked closer.

"What's he say?"

"What's the matter with him?"

"Aw, is he going to throw up now that we've landed?"

Luke's smiling false face widened. "No. We'll come, right behind you."

"If you're sure."

"I'm sure. Thanks."

With the soldiers' backs finally to them, Luke turned to his clan brother. Nantai's flickering eyelids were closed. Luke reached into his jish bag and took out the bone he'd found at the ancient cliff dwelling when he was twelve. He dipped the bone into his small abundance of corn pollen and marked a circle on Nantai's forehead. "Eagle People," he chanted softly in Dinè. "Welcome my brother back to earth. He has two eyes, two ears, two legs, and a true heart, like you. Help him find his balance on the ground."

Nantai's eyes opened slowly.

"Better?" Luke asked.

Nantai grunted. "You sing well, College Boy."

"Thank you."

"But that's a turtle bone."

"I know." Luke sniffed. "Who better to welcome you back to earth than one so grounded?"

"I did not consider that."

"Well," Luke drawled out slowly, "you have not been to college."

Outside the airplane's window Luke saw Jack Spencer, dressed in deep black, clothing that looked like what the *belegaana* wore in mourning. Was this part of their welcome? A death custom?

Luke looked past Spencer and over the concrete-covered field. A black automobile sat on the edge of the lighted area. Stop thinking in this way, he told himself. Almost all automobiles were black. They were not being surrounded by death and mourning. A flash of red, suddenly, like a bird on the wing caught his attention, beautiful. Welcoming. He stood in the aisle of the plane, waiting for his clan brother to get to his feet.

As the door opened, Luke felt the frosted air, so different from winter air at home, so full of what? Water. They descended the metal stairway to the tarmac.

Mr. Spencer's coat swirled like a whirlwind as he approached. Luke remembered to thrust out his hand to greet their head shepherd in the *belegaana* manner. Not their salute, though Spenser was a superior in the service. But this was a different kind of service, one with no saluting, and no uniforms.

"Welcome to New York, gentlemen!" Jack Spencer's brows knit as he considered Nantai. "Airsick?"

"Maybe a little, sir. But he'll be all right," Luke answered for his clan brother too quickly, too loudly.

"Of course. I wish I could give you a longer layover, even show you some of our city's sights, but since Pearl, we need to act fast. See how many of our hare-brained schemes work, you know? Playing tourist? Well, that can wait until your return."

"Yes, sir."

Their superior continued talking as they walked together down the airstrip. "I've been reading the reports filed by your officers during basic training. They are extraordinary. Your marksmanship is exceptional: both sharpshooter grade. And your survival skills over those four days in the Mojave... I believe they're convinced you've got camel blood, the way you store water."

Luke felt his clan brother's nudge, and was glad Nantai's humor was returning. They had never confessed about cutting into the cacti when their canteens went dry. Perhaps these people didn't know where to find water in a desert because they were used to places like this, where the water was in the very air they breathed.

Spencer addressed Nantai. "Lieutenant Riggs, exactly what kind of relation is Lieutenant Kayenta to you?"

"We are brothers born to the Salt Clan, sir."

"Brothers? But your last names are not the same."

"Cousins," Luke tried a name the *belegaana* used, but the Dinè did not. "We are distant cousins."

"I see," Spencer said.

Luke was not sure he had explained it well enough, so perhaps Spencer was being polite.

"Well, you are now our clan brothers in this crazy branch of the service."

"Yes, sir," Nantai said.

"Thank you, sir," Luke followed the pattern they practiced during training, a pattern that seemed to please their military trainers, who addressed their Navajo "chiefs" as one, and sometimes treated them as if they were a long and shorter version of the same being.

Jack Spencer smiled, but Luke could see that this *belegaana* would never mistake one of them for the other. His eyes reminded Luke of a hawk's in flight.

Wind kicked up around them. Luke tied the belt of his coat tighter, telling himself he was not avoiding a whirlwind spirit, he was just cold.

The closer sight of a couple, now sitting beside the black automobile he'd noticed from the airship's window, distracted him. The flashing red bird's welcome was really the woman's shoes.

Spencer slowed his stride. "Family farewells. Always difficult," he said. "Captain Charente's your pilot. He'll be flying you out tomorrow. He'll be one of your instructors, too, over there."

They were in their own world; the shining man sitting on the running board, the woman in the passenger seat above him, dressed in deep blue like a portion of this night's sky, her shoes the color of heart's blood. Music drifted out of the car's radio, the melody from a more metallic instrument than the flutes of Luke's homeland, but towards the same purpose — casting a spell of longing. The couple seemed as beautiful and distant as the stars from which Luke had descended.

The woman pulled her man close. Her fingers sifted through his hair.

With that gesture, the gap between them evaporated. His mother and grandmother held

Luke like that the day he left, so that he would not see their tears. But he'd felt them in his heart. Did Red Shoes Woman feel the same for her man? Luke felt struck, then oddly comforted by the echo of his own women's mourning.

Chapter 2

Eaton Manor, England
January 20th 1942

Luke wondered if pouring another glass of the potent Scotch whiskey into the potted plant would harm it. He did not know its name, but its long pointed leaves looked almost as dangerous as the bristling old weapons mounted on the walls around him — swords and daggers, shields, muskets and armor. Where was Nantai? There, across the next room, the one the owners called the Great Hall. His clan brother had found Captain Charante among the antlers and the portraits of generations of hunters that lined the walls. He should try to join their conversation, Luke decided, even if the airman was talking about his wife.

But before he reached them, someone slammed Luke in the back. It was Tillerson. "Hey, Chief! You bull's-eyed our target on every jump! So what I want to know is this — why you and your little shadow aren't on our team for going into France? What are they going to do with your big chief fighting skills? Your quick-study Morse code and semaphore skills? And we could sure use your ways around using and fixing radios! So, why do you two have a different first mission? Any ideas?"

Luke put on his false-face smile for the large mouthed man. "As I understand it, our assignments are not our choice, sir."

"Sir? Sir? We don't have to be 'sir-ing' each other here! Now, we're new-minted graduates... all officers! Even the two of you, imagine that?"

"It is hard to imagine," Luke agreed quietly, careful not to step back, though Tillerson reeked of strong drink, and Luke wanted to get away from him.

"Don't know what the service is coming to. Peeling potatoes, shining boots, fine. Entertaining us even. But intelligence work? I mean, you people still live in teepees, don't you?"

"The Dinè never did."

Don't say too much. Stay quiet. This man doesn't desire any knowledge about the ways of the Dinè. Luke looked across the room — desperate. There. The airman, Philippe Charente. Coming toward him, his hand outstretched in rescue.

"Cecily Barker has been looking for you," he said over his shoulder to the drink-soaked Tillerson. Then he steered Luke toward his clan brother.

Once the three of them gathered around a marble table placed under the portrait of the 4th Duke of this place, Captain Charente continued, in that quiet voice which reminded Luke of his Uncle Ahiga. "Keep your eyes on Tillerson, my friends. Let us see if he will tell Cecily what she's instructed to get out of him. Were I a betting man, I would say he will be out of our service before midnight."

"But we have all graduated, Captain," Luke said.

"*Mais non,* not quite, that is. This soiree is the last test. Tillerson is clever and has been lucky. But I do not think he will survive Cecily combined with *in whiskey veritas.* He will let something confidential go to gain her favor, and will be dismissed."

Nantai shook his head. "Why do you tell us this, Captain Charente? If what you say is true, then we have not yet graduated, either."

"You? You, my friends, have the sense to remain sober, without even the watchers catching on. Why, even Wild Bill Donovan's job, it is not safe from you two!"

Nantai smiled. "From you, sir, I think, if you caught us staying sober."

Captain Charente's grin widened. "Come, let's find some chairs and sit down, my friends. My wife has sent fresh photographs. Let me show you the beach at Coney Island."

Nantai rolled his eyes before the three of them grabbed gilt decorated side chairs and placed them around the table. Luke smiled weakly, as the airman continued. "When we return home, we will all go out together! We will get the best fish, right off Sheepshead Bay. There, see?"

The airman held up a photograph of boats at a dock, and behind it, a long building with a tile roof that looked long and wide enough to hold all the people of Arizona under it. "We'll have clam chowder and huckleberry pie! See?" He flicked the side of a photograph with his finger. "There is my best girl with her brother Matty."

Luke nodded at the handsome couple with matching smiles holding up enormous wedges of pastry. "Oh, my Kitty will love you two," Captain Charente said, "A taste for adventure and the exotic, she has. What else drew her to me, eh? A game girl, as they say in the States, full of *joi de vivre*, that is how my people, the Quebecois express it. How is it said out West?"

Nantai frowned. "There is no need to say something like that. All of our women are brave, and full of life."

The airman threw back his head and laughed.

Luke was glad Charente had taken no offense, but wondered what had his clan brother in such a talkative mood. They were both more comfortable with the Canadian airman. Maybe that was it. Or maybe Nantai had not poured all of his own whiskey into spiked potted plants.

"My Kitty is loyal, like you two are to each other," Captain Charente said. "She will blend you into that family of hers, just as they have swallowed me."

Why was a man so in love with his wife and her family in this dangerous branch of the service, Luke wondered again. Their other instructors talked about past successes in their service as they demonstrated the use of miraculous scientific gadgets. Even in their off-duty hours, those men spoke of the importance of coming missions.

All except for the French-Canadian airman, who only talked of coming home.

Charente pointed to another of his white serrated edged photographs. "There she is in the surf with her sister. Mermaids in the water, the two of them are, trained in the swimming by their brothers. Joe, Matty, Michael and Dominic, who were lifeguards at the beach every summer. The Mama and Papa Berry, they made good children, and they all make room for me as well!" He glanced up quickly. "Already taken, the sister Anya is. You've got to act quickly with the Berry girls. Loyalty and those legs, eh? A good combination!"

It was not the taller sister who pulled Luke into the photograph, but the beautiful legs and radiant smile of the airman's wife.

Chapter 3

Vicente, Spain
February 22, 1942

Manchego, hotelier and postmaster, filled up the doorway of the Rhamah Café. A passing waiter alerted him to the presence of "one of Spencer's Mexicans." A mistaken assumption, but the *belegaana* of America sometimes thought Luke and Nantai were Mexican too, because of their dark skin, and the kind of spoken Spanish they learned from the descendants of the conquistadors. The Mexicans were still some of the Dinè's trading partners in sheep and wool, so he and Nantai had learned the language from them.

The weekly dance between Luke and the Spanish mountain town's chief began. Manchego nodded in Luke's direction, both his eyebrows and mustache lifting. Luke returned the silent acknowledgement. The hotelier then left the wooden beam and tiled dining room. Attention drifted back to midday meals of the men, with Basque and French words peppering conversations at the small round tables.

As Luke finished his crab-rich paella, Manchego reappeared. He had replaced his plain wool cap with a feathered, flat topped felt one, signifying his transformation into a government official. He carried two frayed parcels in his hand. Luke surmised that the now postmaster general wasn't going to give up his guest's mail without a ceremony. And without some information to further fuel the town's curiosity about the strangers in their mountains.

"Released from your solitude today? But without a glass of our fine wine?"

Luke smiled. "Might you report such an indulgence, *el administrador de correo*?"

"Indulgence? *Dios!* More likely I'll report to Señor Spencer that you do not support Vicente's fragile economy! Tell me this much at least, my sober friend. How did Señor Spencer's fine flock of Churra fare in the last storm?"

Luke's smile widened at this turn in their conversation. "All are thriving, thank you."

"And the three wonders of the canine world that I found for you? They are serving you well?"

"The dogs know how to tend and protect our flock, as they find fresh grazing spots by day, sir. They are indeed wonders."

"When our men went off to fight in the wars, these ancient breeds, I think they looked after our sheep alone! Shall I tell your Señor Spencer that you and your brother shepherd are not required at all? That he only needs to feed the *Can de Palleiro*, the golden *Gorbeikoa*, and their more hairy companion?"

"Please do not let our boss in on this secret, sir."

25

"Ah well. The sheep do not receive interesting packages from across the Atlantic, around which we invent stories! They do not buy rice and olives and walnuts! And the Churra, are they milking well?"

"We don't milk them."

"Oh? It is not as some of our village fear then? That the wealthy Señor Spencer is experimenting with putting our *Quesucos* and *Serrat* cheese makers out of business?"

"Mr. Spencer's interest is in the sheep's wool, sir."

"Ah, the wool! A good choice, the Churra. Though some, like the English, are more particular in their breeding and will have only the Merino. Imagine! Have you had a first shearing?"

"We have, with only a few, as it is still so cold in the mountains. I have brought some fleece in hopes you might know of someone who might weave a sample rug to send to Mr. Spencer."

Luke opened the sack at his feet and revealed the variety of long fibers of apricot, gray, black, brown, beige and white. They left the town's postmaster momentarily speechless.

"This is a fine grade, and well washed. You and your partner can shear and clean as well as a shepherd, then! And this puts to rest one rumor — that your employer, cut off from his perfume ingredients by war, is more interested in gaps in the mountain border with France."

Luke thought of a way he could tell the truth. "Mr. Spencer is dedicated to his sheep."

"So this wool proclaims. Donata!" Luke's host called out in a bass voice that matched his size.

A young woman in a yellow-flowered dress and worn blue apron appeared.

"My daughter is an excellent spinner, Señor Kayenta." He opened his hand. Donata placed hers in her father's palm. "Can you see that she is no stranger to the trade?"

The woman's hands reminded Luke of those of his grandmother, his mother, his sisters — supple from contact with lanolin, and strong.

"And Donata weaves rugs of a most artistic design," her father continued.

Donata had not spoken. Even the dark braids, looped and tied back behind her ears were still. What did she think of what was being bartered without her consent, Luke wondered. This would never happen at home. Dinè women owned the sheep. Weaving was their domain, every aspect of it controlled by them. But he was not home. And he needed the postmaster's daughter to help tame rumors of illegal activities, of smuggling French perfume or worse, refugees from Vichy France in over the mountains.

Manchego pulled Donata closer.

"Will you allow her to turn this wool into a pleasing product for Señor Spencer's enterprise?"

"I would be glad to, Señor Manchego," Luke said quietly, looking up at the girl's face. She smiled quickly, brightly, as her looped earrings moved. But what was her expression just before she knew his eyes would meet hers? Something that reminded Luke of an animal baring its teeth. Or did he see enemies everywhere?

Her smile turned languid as Manchego continued to praise her skill. When he sent her into the kitchen for wine to toast their agreement, the sway of her hips was echoed by her full skirts.

Manchego kicked back his chair, swelling his barrel chest before his patrons.

"My friends and neighbors! Your attention, if you please! *Señor* Kayenta has engaged my household in his employer's new enterprise— to have all of America standing proudly on fine Churra wool rugs! Please join us in a toast to the partnership!"

They were partners now?

Each diner drank to their success. Their glasses were quickly refilled by the hotelier's returning daughter. Manchego thumped Luke's glass with his own, splashing the wine over his fingers. Luke fought the lurch of nausea, and drank.

The men crowded around them, speaking too fast for him to catch every word. Manchego cleared them more space with a swipe of his big hand. Luke wished he were back in the mountains with his dogs, his sheep. In Dinetah the Spanish Churra sheep were now called Churro and had been friends of the people since the conquistador Coronado came looking for the fabled Cities of Gold. The Spaniard's conquering army traveled with the beautiful, long-faced flocks. Raiding and trading for them and for the Spanish horses changed the life of the Navajo people forever.

"Stand back, my friends," Manchego commanded now. "*Señor* Kayenta has yet to receive this very important postal delivery from the honorable and excellent *Señor* Spencer!" His voice only went down a notch in volume. "Allow me to present them to you."

At last the parcels reached Luke's hands.

As Manchego enjoyed the attention of his neighbors, Luke slipped through the swinging doors of the café, into the small lobby of the hotel.

Donata was waiting, holding his coat, his knapsack full of food and supplies. He was not yet free.

"*Señor Timido*," she said in a soft teasing voice, taking hold of his outstretched hand then pressing it over the curve of one breast.

"I would put the perfume you bring to me here," she said. "The one the French call Armorial, yes? Might I have that one?"

He willed his hand motionless, though he couldn't control his lower reaction. They were not close enough for Donata to feel that, though her eyes said she knew, and was enjoying his embarrassment.

Why is she doing this?

He waited. Her expression changed.

"Should I forever smell like cooking grease and sheep?" she demanded, before her look turned sly. "Or perhaps I should be content to accept old bottles of Tai-Tai from our German guests? Four of those guests this morning, so curious about you, and your waiting mail."

"Opened?" he asked.

"Not this time."

"The perfume you favor... Armor—?"

"Armorial. Not in the shops since the Germans took Paris. But your Señor Spencer could pack an ounce secure in your next mail pouch, I think. He is an important man, no? And so very rich. Will you remember to ask for it?"

"Yes."

"You do not hold wine well, I think."

"I think you are right." He'd been instructed to tell the truth, whenever he could, he remembered again. It made the lies more plausible.

"But, after our potent wine, still so virtuous. You must have a sweetheart."

Pouting, she released his coat.

Luke placed the parcels against his chest, before yanking the zipper closed and turning up the sheepskin collar. The packages would be safe inside his short workman's coat with its wide snug waist band. He pulled on his knapsack and hat and stumbled out into the winter afternoon.

He looked up Vincente's main street, feeling dizzy from Donata, her information, and the wine. He remembered where his last letter from Jack Spencer had instructed him to open these packages; the church.

* * *

Out of the busy town square and blowing wind, Luke was deeply grateful for the quiet within the stone structure's profound silence. Once his eyes adjusted to the candlelit darkness, he scanned the interior. Not open, or round, like a hogan or sweat hut at home. He felt blind in places like this, unable to see around so many corners. Why had Jack Spencer sent him into these shadows?

To hide, of course. Where so much could be hidden, he might also hide.

He breathed easier.

The main altar was ahead and shone bright with banks of colored glass-surrounded candles. Upon the raised marble altar was gold, the metal that the *belegaana* went crazy to acquire. Luke was glad he wasn't to sit near there. Mr. Spencer instructed him to go into one of the shadow places — an east-facing side chapel. Luke found it and the person of honor next to its smaller modest wooden altar. She was different from the lady nestled in roadside shrines at home. This was not a richly dressed Virgin of Guadalupe, with rays of sunlight encircling her, and an angel and moon at her feet. This was a simply clad young mother with her suckling infant fashioned out of plaster and paint. Luke felt somehow protected here — by the statue, by the cool stone floor and the sound of flowing water. He sat in a high-backed pew and opened the first parcel — the one containing his letters from home.

Home came alive in the dense blue writing of his women. His mother Lillie wrote for her mother, Grandmother Anaba, who did not speak or write in English, but who was a keeper of stories, including one she remembered from her childhood — the 1864 Long Walk, when Kit Carson and his soldiers had driven the Navajo into a long exile. Lillie wrote that his grandmother reminded him to be brave over this exile, as he had been over his own time at his Fort Defiance boarding school, and during the Great Livestock Massacre.

Luke shook his head. His boarding school at Fort Defiance had been a time of heartbreak and loneliness, away from his family. But his sisters Ada and Judith had made his way better by teaching him a few *belegaana* words and phrases to appease the harsh teachers and matrons who only spoke English to their students, leaving them confused and bewildered. And Ada and Judith protected him when they could, from the bigger boys when they tried to push him down or steal his pennies or Christmas candy.

He was not as brave of those who endured punishments worse than his own. And he wasn't any help at all during the Livestock Massacre, which took place after he had completed three years at Fort Defiance and was home for the summer. He was singing a soothing song as Grandmother untangled a lamb from a sticker bush when the federal men came with their flatbed truck, their bulldozer, their liquid fire. Luke proudly translated their orders to gather up all but three-hundred of their flock, and place them in the deep trenches their bulldozers had made. "Why are they doing this, Grandson?" Anaba asked.

He tried. He tried to find the right words to ask them in English. One of the men began to talk about topsoil, and stock reduction requirement and the ways of the new leaders in Washington. But Luke couldn't follow his too-fast speech. Another man shoved the first one aside. "To count, only, don't worry. You know the federal people. They are always counting." Is that what he had said? And when his grandmother hesitated, that's when the one in charge took Luke's shoulder in his grip. He smelled like death. "Tell her if she protests, she will go to jail."

Luke should have known. He should have understood their English better. But he was only ten years old, and so interested in the bulldozer, in the different and interesting turn this day had taken. He should have read the worry on Grandmother's face. She knew these people. She had survived the Long Walk.

33

By the time the workers blocked one end of the trench, his mother and sisters had come and stood beside him and Grandmother. They all watched, faces frozen in disbelief as the men doused their animals in gasoline. Then one of them flicked a match into the trench. Luke covered his ears, buried his head in his mother's skirts, but could still hear the pitiful bleats of the sheep, the screams of the goats as they burned. Animals that had names, animals who trusted his family. Half their herd burned to death before their eyes that day.

Luke did not want to return to the boarding school after that. He wanted nothing to do with white people. But Grandmother asked him to. She said she had had a dream. Dreams were important, and their messages should be considered. She said he was wearing his grandfather's army uniform from the Great War in her dream. He was standing on a bridge of rainbow light. She wanted to live to tell stories of how he became his holy name, He Understands, and formed bridges of understanding between them and the *belegaana.*

So, he continued. And helped the biologist with his research about life in the dessert around Fort Defiance. And that man sponsored Luke's studies at the University of Arizona. Men came to his college after this new war began to offer him a place in their fighting force. Mr. Spenser was one of them. They were looking for men who could speak fluent Navajo and English. Fearless men, they said, who could train as soldiers, and learn new weapons, new tools of war. Men like himself and his clan brother Nantai, who helped him gather samples of the Desert Rat for his teacher, the biologist, to study. If they proved themselves, they would become the teachers of more Navajo. Navajo who would help their country win the war.

Luke explained all this to their women, for counsel. His grandmother spoke for them. "You are warriors," she said. "Our homeland has been invaded. She needs warriors to protect our sacred mountains and all that lies in between. You must remind these men that you are Americans, the way your grandfather did. Tell them that this land, America, that we all walk on is our Mother."

His sisters' eyes were shining with unshed tears. His mother stood very tall and straight. She said only. "Take your grandfather's watch. It will help you understand their ways."

Luke continued reading his letters from home. His sisters had married good husbands who treated them with respect. They each wrote to him in beautiful painted word pictures of the winter in their mountains. Judith's rugs and baskets were fetching good prices in Babbit's Trading post. Her small sons Burke and Teddy were already helping with their flocks.

From his closer in age sister Ada, Luke read of his niece Iris's First Laugh ceremony. "It looks like this one has decided to stay with us, my brother." His sister did not have to say he should have been there. As uncle of a child he'd yet to see, he had duties, responsibilities. He was part of his mother's and sisters' clan. If he had been home, if he had made Iris laugh, he would be hosting her party. He would make sure his niece touched every guest's plate, to show she would be a generous person who shared her food, gifts and laughter with all. Luke was her Shizhé'é Yázhí. And she had already laughed. *Good baby. Bring my sister joy.* Smiling to himself, Luke touched the pocket in the vest over his heart that held the small bracelet he'd hammered out of melted British silver coins on the day he'd learned of her birth. Why did he craft it? Because it was her Laughing Day gift. But how would the gift honor her if he knew no one to give it to in her name, in the way of the Dinè, to honor his niece? He was failing at his first duty towards her, towards his clan. He tried to suppress an ache of loneliness the thought touched off in him.

Luke imagined slipping the bracelet over the small wrist of Captain Charente's wife, her eyes glowing, the deep love he'd witnessed on the airstrip for him, not her husband. He saw again the shape of her thigh through her night-sky dress. The feel of soft breast became hers, not the recent memory of Donata's invitation.

Stop it. These are not good thoughts in a church.

And the pilot had been kind to them. Philippe Charente had flown them across the Atlantic, and trained them in the countryside castle estate outside ravaged London. He'd taught them how to use instruments and weapons that were often hidden inside other, more common things — a boot brush holding a fuse, a watch face with a message encoded, a clothesline wrapped around a radio antennae.

The captain praised them over each new accomplishment, like the most patient of teachers. Like a Navajo, not like their harsh boarding school matrons and teachers. Luke and Nantai learned about the new things the English were making better than the Americans. They were smaller and more cleverly hidden tools. The English had been at war and in the spy business longer than the Americans.

But at night Philippe Charente had shown them too many photographs of his woman. The images showed her laughing, dancing, and in hats decorated with ribbons and netting and flowers. They'd traded good stories of courtship and families and hunts — Philippe's in the skies, theirs in the canyons.

Thinking of stealing his wife was not a way to thank the airman, even if Philippe Charente didn't have enough sense to stay close to a woman so full of life.

He should make amends, Luke decided, before his contact found him here. He should pray for the beautiful couple he'd seen sitting out among the stars.

He looked up at the painted statue and found a ready forgiveness in the mild eyes of the little mother. Something was written below her small feet. Luke couldn't understand the words; they were not etched in the Spanish language. Who was she?

"Our Lady of the Good Delivery and Bountiful Milk," a voice answered his unspoken question. "In Latin: *Lacte et bene parerent Dominae Nostrae* it sounds like poetry, does it not?" The gentle click of wooden rosary beads came late, as if the tall, bearded brown-robed man had somehow floated to his place beside Luke.

"The Mother of God has many names, yes?" the priest said in beautifully modulated English. "Our town's women favor this one, and this small chapel dedicated in her honor. Welcome, Mr. Spencer's American shepherd."

"Mikolas," Luke whispered.

"Father Mikolas, yes. And I am ready to assist you with providing the names of your new flock. Our church is built over a spring. We baptize the children in it now, See?" He gestured toward the marble baptistry carved with babies with small wings growing out of their backs, like fledgling eagles. "The church calls it holy water now, but it has always been sacred. This is a chapel for the women, the children. But sometimes the oppressed come here also, to bathe in our waters. They emerge transformed — with identification papers, passports, visas."

Luke smiled. This thin man with large expressive eyes was truly the agent Mikolas, then. Their other OSS contacts were all republicans. He hadn't been expecting a priest.

Most clergy had been loyal to the dictator Franco in Spain's civil war.

Father Mikolas' voice grew more concerned. "The prison between here and San Sebastian, is called Porta Coeli. It was once a holy place for our religious brothers, but it has been a fortress of a prison for many years. And it has never been so strong as it is now. Generalissimo Franco is very hard on opposition thinkers." His mouth quirked up in a gentle smile. "But, although expression and action may be deemed criminal, thought is free, is it not?"

This was possible Luke told his doubts. There were priests like this one in his own country, ones who cared about injustice and the poor more than complicated theology or the grandness of their own churches.

"The prison has doubled its guards since the bombing at Guernica," Mikolas continued. "Those who venture near, they tell of the screams carried on the wind. Each mother, daughter, wife and sister of prisoners imagines the screams belong to her own loved one.

"These, the women, are your strongest supporters. They have guided many refugees over our mountains. They tear labels from clothes to sew into foreign garments so the strangers blend in. These women wonder, if, once the ones on your list are found, that other cells might be opened?"

Luke inhaled deeply. "Father, I am only a bridge person. Not any mission's planner or leader. I can promise nothing."

"Not even to explain that the ones in other cells, they come from here, they know this land? And that they are willing to help guide your own people to the sea?"

This priest had good bargaining skill. "Well," Luke drawled in the slow-talking fashion of the Dinè to honor it, "I can do that much, yes."

Suddenly, Father Mikolas's nostrils flared. He gripped Luke's shoulder, looking out beyond. *What is wrong?*

The priest spoke loudly, switching to Spanish. "Are you ready, my son?"

"*Si, padre*," Luke replied calmly, though his veins felt ignited. What was he supposed to be ready for? He stood and followed where Father Mikolas pointed— behind the heavy red curtain of the confessional.

Within its confines, Luke's fear intensified. He didn't want to die in a place like this, scented with centuries of incense, hair pomade and guilt. He knelt. He had not confessed his sins to a priest since he was twelve, when the Protestant missionaries granted his next educational step, with the strings of the practice of their brand of Christianity attached, thereby continuing his lifelong confusion about the nature of Christianity.

"Give up nothing their medicine people offer you," his Grandmother Anaba had advised. "Add your knowledge of their ways, their Jesus and Moses, their stories, their Mass and their priests and ministers. Some things will connect to our ways, our stories. Other things will not. Add all to your quiver. Try to understand them. But act like the People, always."

Father Mikolas settled beyond the latticed partition. He slid open the small amber window between them. At the sound Luke jumped reflexively, just as he had as a boy.

"Bless me, Father, for I have sinned," he said, surprised by how familiar the words still felt on his lips.

Silence. Confusion. Fear. His own, or the priest's? Was someone listening, even here? No more talk of the mission, then, or the prisoners of Porta Coeli. Wait, Luke told his racing heart. Wait for the priest to lead him.

Through the dim yellow light he saw Father Mikolas place a purple stole around his neck. "So. Is there something you wish to tell me, my dear shepherd?" he asked gently.

He was a shepherd again. Not a soldier getting crucial names and numbers from a local contact. What to tell? Luke asked both the chapel's patron and the holy spring to help him.

"I have... a heartsickness, Father."

No, that was how he'd tell a medicine person his trouble, not a priest. Luke took another breath and searched for the *belegaana* way of expressing it. Think. Which of the Christian commandments was he breaking? "I covet another man's wife."

"I see. Have you had carnal relations with this woman?"

"No."

41

"But she has enticed you with her charms?"

"No! This does not belong to her, only to me."

In the dim light, Luke thought he saw the priest tamp his lower lip with a long finger as he considered. "Well, ask the Virgin Mary to help you with these feelings."

"The little mother of this chapel?"

"Yes, the little mother... of God."

Good advice, Luke decided. "Thank you, Father."

"Now. Please recite an act of contrition, while I absolve you of all your sins."

"O my God, I am heartily sorry for having offended Thee..." Luke remembered the words to that prayer too, and, to his own amazement, after saying them, while resting his fingers on the leather strings of his jish pouch, he felt both calmed and cleansed. He resolved to place his wishful images of the airman's wife in a far corner of his heart.

Father Mikolas removed his stole and kissed its ends, whispering. "Now. Let us allow those German soldiers on leave — the ones in the back pew of the chapel of the little Mother? Let us give them a good look at you receiving Holy Communion. They are Catholic. So they know that if they shoot you now, they will be creating a saint."

That's what had made the brave priest go pale, then, Luke realized. The sight of soldiers on holiday entering a woman's side chapel on a weekday afternoon.

"Father Mikolas, why do you help us?" Luke asked impulsively.

"You noticed the brightness of our main altar?"

"I did," he admitted.

"It is not gilded wood, my dear shepherd. It is solid gold, forever bright. And it was taken from the New World, from your Americas, at unconscionable cost, by my ancestors. Still, you Americans now come to help us, here in the Old World at a time of great peril. Most astonishing of all, two of the Native people, who we wronged most grievously, are here. So, we can help you and redeem ourselves. Who would not jump at this opportunity?"

"Many would not, Father."

"Many have not. Keep all your senses alert, Luke. To those outwardly pandering, as well as the outwardly hostile. Friends lurk beneath each. As do enemies."

Luke felt the priest's smile. "So, it seems we have had twin confessions, a clearing of both our souls here in this sacred space. Though my sin is not nearly as interesting as yours."

"Father, the names?" Luke drew him back to their business.

"Ahead. That communion of souls is ahead," he promised, "provided you survive outside this confessional's sanctuary." He stood and left the small space.

Luke rose from the kneeler, pushed aside the heavy velvet, and followed the priest to the side chapel's altar. He knelt at the railing while

43

Father Mikolas reached into the tabernacle. He held a gold chalice high.

Luke prayed to the small woman to help keep him on a good path, to be a good friend to Nantai, to help him bear his own loneliness on his separate mountain perch.

Father Mikolas turned, and then placed a wheat-flecked host on his tongue. Luke hadn't fasted, so Holy Communion did not taste sacred. It tasted like bread, mixing with the paella remnants in his mouth.

Father Mikolas spoke in softly rolling Latin as he covered Luke's head with one hand. With the thumb and finger of the other hand, he made the imprint of small crosses on his forehead, then lips, then over his heart. It was very like a Medicine Person's corn pollen ceremony and it left Luke in a spell of deep peace.

"I have given you the shepherd's absolution from attending Mass," the priest explained. "God knows you are doing His work in the mountains."

"My brother Nantai is, too," Luke said.

The priest smiled. "Nantai is included, of course."

"Thank you, Father."

"I give you a deacon's duty now, my young friend — that of delivering the sacrament to your fellow shepherd."

Father Mikolas returned to the small altar's tabernacle, placing a linen wrapped host into a round glass receptacle. He positioned that in the depths of a silk-lined rosewood case. Luke heard the Germans shift in their seats behind him. He hoped Father Mikolas had hidden the mission's names well within as he accepted the box.

He placed it beside his grandfather's watch and his niece's bracelet over his heart. He turned.

The soldiers, dressed as mountain climbing tourists, one in a tweed coat, the other in corduroy, seemed absorbed by the sight of a gray dove flying fruitlessly against the painted blue sky of the church ceiling. Luke stepped up his pace. He saw the boot jut into the aisle too late.

The marble baptismal font broke his fall.

A flood of German that sounded like an argument between the two was quickly joined by Father Mikolas's Spanish protests. As Luke rose, the Germans took him under his arms and dragged him outside and down the side steps of the church.

The men smelled of Patxaran, that potent liquor that Manchego served in the cafe. That fact gave Luke a smattering of hope — perhaps they were only bored and drunk, not acting out orders. He had endured a few beatings at boarding school. He could endure this. But then he caught another, strong scent, the same hair pomade that was within the confessional. Had one of them already invaded that sacred space, perhaps searching for what Luke now had?

The town square, so busy when he'd entered, was deserted, the shops facing the church shuttered. On the uneven stone street, hands tore the knapsack from his back. A booted foot held his shoulder down, while the other German's hand rifled into his clothing, complaining. *About what?* He smeared his hand across Luke's collar. A splotch of red. Maybe the complaint was about his blood, despoiling the very white hand, the cuffs of his expensive mountaineering suit. The German found, yanked out the wooden box from his inside vest pocket. He flung it open. Too hard. The glass holder smashed onto the cobblestones.

Silence followed as the sacred Eucharistic Host, now only wrapped in the small cloth of white linen, descended into a gutter.

Even the louder of the two Germans, the one who'd caused Luke to fall against the baptismal font, looked on in silence.

With his almost noiseless walk, Father Mikolas reached the gutter and carefully rewound the fabric around the Body of Christ. He approached Luke and knelt beside him, tucking the sacred package into his vest.

"Return to your sheep," he said quietly, in English.

Collecting the emptied box, Father Mikolas surrendered it to Luke's tormentors. They examined it, arguing with each other. Though the soldiers flanked the priest, it was Father Mikolas who seemed in charge of two recalcitrant, light-haired choir boys, who had desecrated a sacred object. They finally issued what Luke surmised was a gruff apology. Father

Mikolas was having none of it. He led them back into the church. *For their own confession?* To Luke's amazement, they followed, and he was left alone in the small square.

Luke leaned over, dizzy and coughing more blood onto the cobblestones. Rise up, he told himself, get on the mountain road. But the blood flowed over the back of his hand.

A girl stood before him, offering his bloodied knapsack. He blinked, focusing on her. She was sad, thin, with beautiful black eyes. Perhaps eight or nine years old. She dragged the knapsack closer, then left it at his feet. She reached into her pocket and found, then raised a handkerchief to Luke's mouth. She pinched his lip's wound between small, strong fingers. Luke tried hard not to cry out or, worse, drop the entire weight of his head between the girl's arms. He breathed in, out.

"*Mi papá*, his name is Arturo Castile," the girl said in practiced, accented English against his ear. "He is in cell number thirty-eight."

Luke reached into his pocket and removed the silver bracelet he'd fashioned. He placed it around the girl's wrist.

"My niece, her name is Iris Wilson, born to the Salt People, born for the Red Ant Clan," he told Arturo Castile's brave daughter. "Here is a gift that honors her. She has just laughed for the first time."

Chapter 4

Luke turned up the oil lamp, illuminating the small second floor living quarters of his home in Spain — a small, wood and mud shelter facing south, that the local people called his *masia*. They used the grand name in jest he thought, because it was the main building of Mr. Spenser's livestock operation, however modest. He started a fire in the hearth.

Out of the cold, his injury began to throb with pain. It could wait. Retrieving his shaving kit from its place beside the water basin, he brought it to his only table.

Luke's practiced hands caused the magnifying glass to spring from its hiding place within his shaving brush. He set the tool down before retrieving the wrapped flatbread Eucharist from his inside vest pocket. The fine linen smelled of starch and the town's cobblestone street. He unwound the disc carefully, placing it in a small blue-flowered ceramic bowl. Then he turned his attention to the cloth, passing his magnifying glass over one side, then the other. Again, looking closer at the weave.

Nothing.

Creeping dread filled his middle. He thought that would be the place. Where were the names?

Luke sat back, clearing his mind with long deep breaths. Outside, the music of the sheep's bells helped him find his balance and breathe more evenly. He remembered what power the sacred bread held over the German soldiers, once they thought their cruelty played a part in its possible desecration. Luke admired its circle shape and letters IHS embossed at the center. He tried to call up what the letters meant, from the Latin of his long ago catechism classes. For once, his iron memory failed him.

The design around the edge of the host was beautiful too, like his mother's fine quillwork.

Was it more than a design? He raised the magnifying glass again, looked closer. The clever needle points formed letters, which made the names of certain imprisoned men of Porta Coeli Prison, each followed by a number. His cell number. "The communion of souls," Father Mikolas had called them. Of course.

Luke searched around the edge, burning all the names and numbers of the prisoners into his mind. He added one more, Arturo Castile, along with what the girl told him, cell thirty-eight.

With his pocket knife he scored the edge of the bread that held the precious information. He broke off the hollowed out hoop and ate it, leaving the center of the host for Nantai. Luke's clan brother had never warmed up to being a Catholic, even when they were children being taught by the priests. But Father Mikolas was a holy man, so that was reason enough to make a gift of it.

Away from the spell the confessional had cast over him, Luke's doubt about Father Mikolas resurfaced. Hadn't the pope himself declared Franco the defender of the Faith for defeating the godless communists of Spain's republic? The inscribed names belonged to republican prisoners, now considered of possible use by the Americans and British for the information they knew, for their wartime fighting experience. He understood that value. But were they not the priest's enemies if they were Franco's and the church's?

Luke sighed deeply, lost again in spirals of suspicion. Nantai was the only one who had his complete trust here. Nantai and the loyal four-legged companions of their twin mountain retreats.

Luke wrapped the sacred host, returned it to the pocket over his heart. He walked to the fire in his open hearth and brewed a pot of his grandmother's sassafras tea.

He let its steam bathe his swollen face before returning to his work stool and resting his feet on the warming stones of the hearth. A soft whine and scratching began at the upstairs door. He knew it was not Lander or Yuli, who had greeted him on his return and now slept content on the first floor. Both medium sized dogs whose flanks reached just above Luke's knees, Lander was a *Can de Palleiro* and Yuli a

Basque breed with a moderate rough coat. Highly intelligent, they loved the sheep and looked after them and the farmstead as well as the smaller, sweet-faced mixed-blood dogs that helped with the Navajo people's herds at home. These two, both golden brown coated, were his hearty fellow workers, fed and enjoying their well-earned rest. Once Luke opened the door, the third dog, the one who herded sheep well but hated the cold nudged his leg.

"All right then, Bodyguard. Come on in and save me from my own cooking," he said.

The dog obeyed, already understanding the Dinè language. Bodyguard was a *Pastor Vasco* with a fluffy long coat that made him look like the sheep. But although his friend did a fine job keeping sheep in line, he thought himself a lapdog once Luke settled in for the night.

Once fed, he barked twice. Luke knew that signal. The dog wanted to hear Bing Crosby singing *Wrap Your Troubles in Dreams.*

Reluctantly, Luke set up the portable gramophone and cranked power into it. He found the record, one of those issued, like the gramophone, by the English secret service. Luke set the needle down, and retreated to his chopping board, wishing Bodyguard had musical taste closer to his own. His sisters wore saddle shoes and sometimes listened to Crosby sing *Pennies From Heaven.* But they had also introduced Luke to the popular American music he liked better — the plaintive ballads of the Carter family and Bo Chatamon. *Wildwood*

51

Flower and *Corrine Corrina* reminded him of the healing chants of his own people, so he liked listening to their recordings. But the English didn't provide any of those.

Luke prepared, then ate his stew slowly, carefully avoiding contact with his injured lip. When juice from the local peppers ran over his wound and made him wince, Bodyguard cocked his curly head.

"And you would have broken my fall and defeated the soldiers in one pounce, I suppose?" he asked.

The dog barked indignant confirmation.

Luke laughed. "Well, then, my brave friend. Next time, we'll leave the sheep with Lander and Yuli, and you'll come down the mountain with me. Just ignore the wiles of Donata Manchego, no matter what tender morsels she offers you."

A protesting bark this time.

Luke grunted back. "If I can, you can. She's offering more than kitchen scraps to me."

Soon Bodyguard, sated by dinner, conversation, and the Crosby croon, lay sleeping by the fire. Downstairs, the other two dogs guarded both Luke and the sheep. He was amazed at how well all three four-leggeds expressed command understanding, fierce devotion and loyalty after so short a time with him.

Luke pulled out his grandfather's watch, opened its golden face to reveal its inner workings. So much trouble to tell time. There was not even a word for time in the Dinè language. In *Dinètah*, you worked on something until it was finished, you met friends around sunset, you talked or danced or sang until the songs were over. But here, he and his clan brother were learning the precision of the hands charting hours, minutes, and seconds. It helped keep them in communication on their separate hills. They practiced their language as Mr. Spenser instructed. Listening carefully, making sure the words they tried out for their coded system were clear, distinct, keeping the emphasis on the correct syllable, listening for changes in tone, in glottal stops that could completely change a word's meaning. Someday, Mr. Spenser told them, their work would mean the difference of life and death for hundreds, maybe thousands.

Nantai would be waiting for his communication now. Luke checked his clothesline-hidden aerial, and removed the wireless equipment from inside the gramophone. He cranked the player towards another purpose — communication, then adjusted the headset. He watched the second hand of his grandfather's watch for the exact agreed-upon moment. Then he began to speak.

"*Gah. Ah-Jah. D-Ah. Shi-Da. Gah. Tsah. Ah-Jah. Be,*" he began, using the Dinè words for rabbit, ear, tea, uncle, needle, ear, and deer to spell out his return.

He frowned, thinking how often vowels appeared in English words. That meant there would be much repetition of the words for ear and ant and ice and oil and uncle. Maybe the code breakers would figure out that those sounds were vowels, without needing to know what they meant, just by their frequency. He must talk to Nantai about this. Perhaps they could remember more than one word for those vowels, to make it harder to decipher.

Luke continued speaking, inviting Nantai to his post the next morning for breakfast, before they split the supplies Luke had bought in town. He signaled nothing of meeting Mikolas or of his trouble with the German soldiers.

Nantai's voice came over the radio waves, answering his transmission. Luke took up a pencil and deciphered the code. One word, translated into its English equivalent, write the first letter of the translation. He read over the results, puzzled.

"Lambs coming in early. Come now. Bring supplies."

Luke sighed deeply. He was so tired. But there was an urgency in his clan brother's tone.

* * *

On board the U-Boat Platka

"Kommandant, we are picking up some odd transmissions."

"Odd? How? Is it in Morse Code?"

"No, sir. Voice."

"In what language?"

"That's just it, sir — we cannot understand the language."

"Basque, no doubt. We are near their territory. The separatists must have found an old wireless set. Report it to the locals. It is hardly our concern."

"But Funkmaat Stahl knows a little of the Basque language, sir. He says that is not what is being spoken. I thought that Herr Adler's proficiency might—"

"Herr Adler is celebrating with the fruits of his latest triumph. He will hardly desire—"

"An intriguing puzzle to solve? That would complete my evening, Kommandant," the U-boat's guest proclaimed behind them.

Helmut Adler followed the young officer through the maze of iron, stumbling once on the way to the radio room. Ignoring the elbow offered, he pulled back the shock of silver at his temple. He must pay more attention to his personal grooming, he decided, as an example to these men, in their own on board world, so far from home. Their camaraderie was commendable. Their anarchist beards were not.

He stumbled again. *Verdammt!* Dark, close quarters of U-boats were not made for his six-foot-three-inch frame. Or perhaps he'd had too much of the champagne retrieved from the freighter's lifeboat.

He frowned, considering that possibility. Why had he raised his glass the third time, toasting to whomever had the presence of mind to salvage such a fine vintage? Because he would have liked to meet a man of such taste. Or woman, he realized with a troublesome pang of dismay, thinking of the beautiful ermine collared coat, blowing, beckoning, before it sank into the depths of the Atlantic.

Is that why he'd thrown so much champagne down his throat? Because there were women killed in the sinking of the Lake Osweya? Never mind. It had nothing to do with him. What madman had allowed women to attempt an Atlantic crossing in the path of the sea wolves? Americans were such soft, stupid people, with their free wheeling walks, their open faces. And they were so untried by war, by years of hardship and humiliation.

Reaching his destination, Adler saw that the radio operator going off duty had written some of what he'd heard on a blue pad. The light was too dim to see the page clearly. But Adler was not going to pull out his monocle, another sign of his forty-four years.

"Good work, *funkmatt*," he complimented, handing him the bottle of champagne. It was always wise to stay on good terms with the crew of a U-boat. Adler sat in the boy's place beside the Enigma machine and signaled for his earphones before adjusting the dial on the long range receiver.

He closed his eyes to concentrate on the scratchy intonations. At first he found only swimming spirals back behind his lids. *Cursed champagne*. He should not have imbibed so much. He must show these men even younger than he was at the start of the last war that he was still fit, still as able as the best of them. And he was seasoned by experience, such hard experience.

Concentrate, he commanded his racing brain. *There.* The crackling voice made images over the spirals. He saw voice patterns, in waves, in colors. That was his gift, a natural gift that his elders had discovered while he was yet a child.

Red. This voice was the red of panic. His own panic, during another war, he realized, in shock. What was happening? Suddenly, he felt thrust back into the Meuse-Argonne Campaign. He was in a muddy trench, in the heat of battle. He was still shy of twenty, struggling with his field telephone, helpless to locate the onslaught of American forces...

"Their position! What is their position?" He heard his captain shout above the unholy din.

"I can't understand what they are saying!" he shouted back, looking up from the strong fingers, fingers still gripping his shoulder hard.

But there would be no more orders. His captain had become a headless corpse.

Listen, Helmut Adler now commanded his stomach, heaving, as his younger self's had when his captain's body crushed down on him. *Come away from there and listen with all your being.* He concentrated on the tone, the pitch, the syllables. Harnessing them within a mind trained to detect nuances, accents, origins; to see sounds.

The sounds began to fit into boxes, each needing to be unlocked. That is the way code is spoken.

"Do you have a way to record this?" he asked the *funkmeister*.

"I could try, sir."

"Do so. Immediately. Before we're out of range. Before they stop."

"They, Herr Adler? Funkmaat Stahl thought it was a single voice. Perhaps an anti-government broadcast."

"Two. There are two voices. We must put in at San Sebastian."

"San Sebastian?" The young Kommandant stood behind him, just as his captain had, in that bloody ditch. "Agent Adler, our destination is Bordeaux."

"I must stay within range. I must explore this transmission further!"

Was that his voice — too fast, edged in panic?

Glances passed between the two officers. The U-boat's captain smiled graciously, but his voice had a steely edge. "We lead the pack, Herr Adler, and are expected in Bordeaux."

Helmut Adler heard himself growl. *Back down.* There will be other paths. If he was careful, and diplomatic.

He forced himself to return a smile to this young man, on his way up, if he could keep his submarine clear of British and American destroyers. "Yes, of course," Adler said calmly, as if his outburst had been a slip of the tongue. "From there I have some transmissions of my own to make, to Berlin." He disliked the self-important tone of his own voice.

"Of course, sir."

"And the recording?" he demanded of the radio petty officer.

The boy checked his devices. "No. I regret to say, they stopped too soon, I could not get a placement. And I believe we are out of range now, sir."

Was that fear edging the *funkmeister's* voice? Fear of displeasing Helmut Adler, senior officer of the Abwehr military intelligence and part of the Fuhrer's working staff? It was Adler's turn to be gracious. "No matter. I heard enough. Thank you so much for your invitation, gentlemen. Most interesting and enlightening. I bid you a good night."

He ripped the scrawled upon paper from its blue pad and tucked it neatly into his belt. Then he threw back his shoulders and stood. "Heil Hitler," he announced.

They responded in kind, though caught off balance by the formality. These were men who trusted their lives to their captain, not the chancellor who was sacrificing their comrades daily for the glory of the Third Reich.

Helmut Adler pulled his jacket closer around his shoulders before he left the radio room, head high, his walk straight.

He had not heard nearly enough to decipher the language, although he recognized its origins — the American West. In his service to the Fatherland between the wars, back when the Abwehr itself was quite illegal, he'd traveled on archeological exchanges. He had learned the rudiments of Cheyenne, Cherokee, Pawnee — the Red Indian languages the Americans used as code in the Great War. He was most proficient in Cheyenne, the language that had caused the German defeat in the Meuse-Argonne Campaign.

But it was a vast continent, full of reservation communities, with a babble of aboriginal tongues. And most of the Red Indians of the American West were not like those in his beloved Karl May novels, Winnetou and his blood brother Old Shatterhand. They were not noble savages, full of dignity. They were poor and dirty, and lived in squalor. At boarding schools the children faced him with fear in their eyes, as if he were trying to trick them when he urged them to speak their language. "English only, English only!" they sang back at him. And their parents were worse: hostile to scientific and linguistic inquiry and distrustful of strangers. He was happy enough to buy their for-the-tourists trinkets, their gaudy silver, their baskets and pots. But would they allow him to enter the spiral, the colors, the tones of their languages? No. They were only free with the nonsense screeching they used to accompany dances they performed for visitors. When he did manage to eavesdrop on them talking their languages with each other, it seemed they were always laughing at him.

Were those two voices experimenting with one of those Red American Indian languages there in the foothills of the Pyrenees, in an officially neutral country?

And did they think themselves safe?

They were not safe. Because he would never again allow the words dancing along the radio wave ether to hold such power over him.

He'd been destined to hear those voices, there on the waves of the Atlantic Ocean. What other explanation could there be? He would find those voices, those men. And they would never do to a German regiment what their Cheyenne comrades had done to his in the harsh winter of 1918.

Chapter 5

All three dogs remained close, which made Luke wary about the stillness around Nantai's sheep station. No sign of the red cloth flag they'd agreed to post within one hundred yards — their trouble warning. Still, Luke stayed to the side of the trail, instinctively reacting to the unnatural silence.

Shapes appeared, barely outlining themselves in the night, circling him everywhere except from behind. He dropped his pack and retreated into the darkness, Bodyguard at his heels.

Signaling Bodyguard, Lander and Yuli to stay low to the ground, hidden, and ready, Luke found a noiseless foothold on a limb of a beech tree, enabling him to climb and disappear out of their sightlines.

The shapes moved forward — five, six, seven, surrounding his abandoned supply packages. He climbed. If he could get high enough, if they continued to tighten their circle, he and the dogs could take them all down. He had just inserted a charged magazine into his Welrod's housing when an exasperated voice pierced the air.

"Aw, you all approached too soon!" a loud voice cut the night air. "We've lost him." The man turned in a wide circle. "Lieutenant Kayenta! Well done, you've bested us. Now, kindly don't shoot any of my men."

Luke maintained his position, and his silence.

"He must be granted clearance, sir," he heard Nantai suggest.

"Oh, right. Let's hear it, then."

Nantai spoke in Dinè, all the words correct. Luke listened closely to the tone. Annoyance, exasperation perhaps, but he detected no coercion.

"What's that mean, exactly?" one of the strangers asked.

Nantai cleared his throat. "The chipmunks join Monster Slayer and Child Born of Water."

"Chipmunks?" one of the shapes below him demanded. "Are we the chipmunks?"

Loud Voice looked up into the tree opposite Luke's. "This is ridiculous! Lieutenant Kayenta, will you please stand down!"

Luke dropped into the lantern's cast circle of light and whistled for the dogs to join him. Of the men, only Nantai faced him. Good. Nantai was the only one Luke wanted to see right now, as he replaced his Welrod with a hand that shook. What he could have done to these foolish men who were not his enemies. He dropped to one knee and buried that hand in Bodyguard's sheep-like fur.

The men laughed nervously, trying to pet the dogs, who growled low at them. Nantai nodded. Understanding, Luke was sure, his anger. Perhaps they were becoming the Monster Slayer Twins of their stories, each needing the other for balance.

A big man with a shock of yellow hair approached, thrusting out his hand. "Good to meet you, Lieutenant. Captain Bob Lomax here. Sorry for the scare. Looks like you've had a long day already." He nodded toward Luke's lip, which was beginning to hurt again.

Luke finally trusted himself to stand. Their eyes met at their matched height, though this captain, his superior, must have outweighed Luke by twenty pounds. And though Captain Lomax's voice remained big, it was not so loud now. "Thanks for bringing home the bacon. My over-eager crew was about ready to put one of your partner's favorite sheep on the spit, eh, boys?"

The men around him laughed and pounded Nantai's back. Luke's clan brother looked as nervous as he'd sounded over the radio. Lander and Yuli flanked him.

* * *

As they finished a meal of salt cod and potatoes, Luke thought of how different these six men crowding Nantai's station were — so full of noise and bluster and challenge.

He learned that only Private Ingrassia, whose father came from Puerto Rico, spoke the Spanish language. How would they fit in? Even dressed in homespun clothing that had been carefully aged into shabbiness, their faces were so open, their walk so free, so without the fear the people of Vicente took in with every breath.

They passed their empty bowls around their circle to Nantai. Then their captain signaled their jostling boisterousness to silence with his big voice.

"First, thanks to our hosts for some fine cooking!" he proclaimed.

"Yeah, you guys know your way around a stew," the red-haired man said.

"Sure beats k-rations," the man whose leg was wrapped in gauze agreed.

"That's better. There's always time to be thankful. Next: Ashton."

The wounded man stood. "Yes, sir?"

"How's your gorgeous gam?"

"Right as rain, sir. Corbett put a sticking plaster on the shin. My parachute made out a lot worse getting tangled in that tree."

"All right, good. Against considerable odds, we all made it, men. And we are now in the good company of our shepherds. Now, you lug-headed chipmunks, class is in session. What's the lesson of your last operation under Lieutenant Kayenta's well-trained dogs and his deadly aim?" Captain Lomax asked his crew.

None answered.

He closed his eyes and took in a long breath like men sitting in *Dinètah* Council sometimes did, before he spoke again. Here's the lesson: "Don't lose your head....To gain a minute...You need your head....Your brains are in it. Got it?"

"Yes, sir," the men replied in one voice.

"What did you say?" Lomax demanded.

"Yes sir!" they echoed, louder.

Their leader nodded his approval. Luke looked over at Nantai, who shrugged, just as mystified by the strange communication between Captain Lomax and his men.

"Hey! You guys got any?" the sergeant, the red-haired man who appeared older than his captain, asked.

"Any?" Luke echoed.

"You know, reciting poems, like on the signs. You know, along the highways at home!"

"We don't know of them."

"Say, where do you two live, that you've never seen the poems on the signs?" the one who introduced himself as Mort the Corp demanded. "You know, sponsored by that shaving cream!"

"We live in Arizona," Nantai said quietly.

"Arizona? Why, Corbett here's from Colorado,. That's close by, ain't it? He taught us quite a few from the signs laid out along U.S. Highway Six."

Luke put a bowl of stewed medlar fruit on the table. "We don't have many vehicles on the reservation. And the roads aren't paved. And, well, we don't shave very often."

"What?"

"Don't shave? What kind of men don't —"

"Indian men of the Navajo nation," Nantai informed them evenly, with a slight flare at his nostrils.

"It's like this," Captain Lomax changed the flow of the conversation away from their differences, "we use what sounds like that crazy shaving cream poetry to help us remember information. We fit the rhymes to our purpose. Say, let's go to work, boys. Lieutenant Kayenta, I believe you have acquired some names and numbers for us to use on this mission?"

"Yes, sir. Twelve, each with a cell number."

"Twelve? That's more than I was led to expect."

Luke thought of the priest's plaintive speech, about other names, other mother's sons. Perhaps Father Mikolas had dimpled some of them onto the sacred bread, along with the official ones. Then there was his own addition.

"All right, the six of us will get the twelve of them out. Those odds are not bad, are they, boys?" Captain Lomax said. "The first?"

Luke remembered the girl with the soulful eyes, hoping to see her father again. "Arturo Castile, cell thirty eight," he said.

Captain Lomax waited until three of his men had their hands raised like schoolboys. He chose one.

Mort the Corp spoke up. "Arturo Castile, you won't have to wait... we're coming to get you... outta cell thirty-eight," he proclaimed.

Their captain smiled. "Not deathless verse, but it will do," Lomax pronounced.

His men signaled their own approval with stomping feet, then repeated the rhyme three times. Three was as sacred a number to the *belegaana* as the four directions were to the Dinè, Luke was learning.

He supplied the other names. His way of remembering them was different — he'd turned each syllable into an image from home. So the name of prisoner Nestor Ajade in cell six became a bird resting ajad; on one leg — while trying to feed six chicks.

Suddenly, Luke's thoughts splintered apart by the piercing sound of a sputtering engine.

Captain Lomax and his men had parachuted in early, yes. But there had been no radio notice of another mission tonight. So this was likely not an Allied sponsored mission. Their guest Americans stared at the open wooden rafters above their heads.

"Please follow my brother down to his root cellar," Luke said.

The men looked to their leader.

"You heard the man," Captain Lomax proclaimed with quiet authority.

So, these Americans could do something quietly, Luke thought. Nantai's mouth quirked, as if he had voiced the observation aloud.

His clan brother cleared a rag rug and lifted the root cellar door. He pulled an English-made flashlight from the kitbag hanging below and tossed it to Luke.

"*Sa'ah naaghai bik'eh hozho*," he said, wishing Luke balance and beauty, in all its complexity, in all of its blessed striving to find the right way in the world.

"Hey, what are you guys saying?" Mort asked.

Both Luke and his clan brother smiled as Luke answered in the way they were instructed to, even to the warriors on their own side. "We're just talking Indian," he said, before leading the men underground.

"Best take the dogs," Luke advised Nantai.

"I will take the two that herd sheep. You take the one who loves you."

Luke slipped into the star-studded night, Bodyguard following.

The whining engine sputtered silent.

He watched the skies between the dark outline of hills. Only a quiet sifting now, wind over wings. There, in the west, he saw the gliding object. He could not make out any markings.

He tried to form a connection with the machine, as he often did with the eagles of his canyons at home. Because in the middle of this bird was life and, he suspected, courage, no matter which side of this war. He did not know if the plane was friend, enemy, or neutral. But the life inside was in trouble. That life could make more trouble for him and the Americans, if the landing was successful. He knew that. But he would face that possibility later. For now, he needed to act in a way that would honor his family. He needed to help.

It circled.

Luke signaled out the open meadow with light.

As the plane turned for an approach, he crossed the air over his head with beams, letting the pilot know where the level land ended in a line of trees. Large, thick trees. The plane advanced toward him, bumping the ground twice. Not slow enough. He signaled his X's harder, though he wasn't sure there was anything the pilot could do to slow the craft down.

He shone the light to his left, a rise of rock, and his right, dense shrubbery. He kept it focused there. The plane turned toward it. Luke heard the branches ripping off.

But no explosion, no fire.

He ran, bid Bodyguard to stay on the ground, and then climbed the battered remains of a sumac that led to the dented door of the cockpit.

He shone his light onto someone seated at the controls, still staring out the windshield at the dense night.

"*L'arreter!*"

Luke blinked. "I'm sorry, I do not understand —"

"It is stopped?"

"Yes."

The pilot turned toward the light of Luke's torch, and smiled. He saw white, dazzling teeth, framed in red lipstick. It was a woman's mouth, and beautiful. And the voice coming from it was shaking, but musical.

"To soften the crash, I apply the brakes while steering alongside an energy-absorbing obstacle. *Voila!* The conservation of momentum principle equals low-energy collision. You will tell him this, yes, the next time he dares call me a crazy woman pilot?"

"Err... sure, Ma'am. Might I help you out now?"

"*Mais oui*, my angel. But we should assist this troublesome man out first, yes?"

Luke shone his light around the small cabin. At the woman's feet was a bloodied man.

"Alain!" she summoned. "Give your hand to our *ange lumiere*."

The man blinked, opened his eyes, and obeyed her command.

Chapter 6

They placed Alain Marius on Nantai's cot. The woman knelt at her man's shoulder. Luke stepped back behind the Americans who crowded into the small room.

Under Captain Lomax's questioning, the woman and battered Frenchman explained the intelligence information they wore hidden in the lining of their clothing, and how they were pursued, their efforts to cross the English Channel thwarted.

Alain Marius looked over the Americans' heads. "Now, if we are cleared as allies, I would like to see your medic, and also the man who carried me in here, please?" he requested.

"That would be Lieutenant Kayenta," Lomax said.

As the men shoved Luke forward, the wounded man gripped his hand. "Yes," he said, "Please, stay, sir."

Marius then turned to the woman. "You see? I have our *ange lumiere* in attendance. You must go and visit with the others. Sing *Lilli Marlen* for these good men, Isabelle."

"Alain —" she protested.

"No bones broken, nothing hit hard except my vanity, yes? My wife knows the song in three languages, gentlemen. She is learning the Russian now, for our latest allies. English version, please, my love. Go now, earn our keep, as I am patched for further travel."

Isabelle's strong, well-cared for hands pressed Luke's shoulder as she rose. Her exotic perfume, designed to send men's heads spinning, did its job, although her vibrant smile in the midst of trouble made him notice more than her beauty.

Luke did as he was told by the band's medic, applying pressure and wiping away blood as Corbett cleaned cuts and found pieces of metal lodged beneath the damaged skin of the man's cheek and scalp. He was a compact man, with light eyes alive with intelligence and curiosity about his surroundings, even through the pain he was smiling through. The water basin darkened red as his broad chest expanded evenly.

Outside their circle, Luke heard Nantai softly stroking chords on his guitar as Isabelle Marius sang in a warm, rich contralto that wound around the melody and filled the small space with longing and beauty.

Her man's suffering eyes lit with pride.

"That Greek queen had only a face. My Isabelle's voice alone can sink ships, yes?"

"And she can land them," Luke reminded him.

"Now, I believe our Lord God himself must have landed our airship, my friend. It is the only explanation that makes sense as I have never allowed her any but a navigator's role in my ships! But you need not tell her I am of this opinion. Women are such sensitive creatures."

Luke did not argue. In his experience, *belegaana* men often underestimated the power of their women.

"Please hurry," the Frenchman urged, "I must see to my plane."

Corbett lifted his head from his task. "Almost done. You've got some hard head, but you need rest, sir," he said.

"Don't worry, I sent our mechanic to look it over," Captain Lomax added.

The Frenchman took hold of his sleeve. "You do not understand. They were in pursuit until the highest altitudes of the mountains. I have put both our operations in danger, captain. We must leave before the border guards estimate where we are down, and you must get out of here as well, for—"

"You'll get your orders radioed in to us, I suspect, Mr. Marius. Till then, I outrank you."

"Outrank?" The man's nostrils flared extravagantly. Why, it is you who are in my service, sir! I am a citizen of the Free French Republic!"

He half rose before his own weakness brought him down on Nantai's cot again.

On the other side of the makeshift curtain, Isabelle Marius completed her song about a soldier's heartbreak in his separation from his loved one.

The men cheered wildly. Her husband closed his eyes at last.

Luke returned to the larger room as Mort the Corp, who was also Mort the Mechanic, ambled into Nantai's quarters, rubbing his hands on an old cloth. Madame Marius slipped into her husband's curtained space. She did not return. When Luke checked in again, she was gone. Her husband slept peacefully. She'd found the small latched door Nantai had fashioned in the wall, driven into the night by the men's recitations of many more of the jingly poetry, Luke suspected. He glanced out the small window. Bodyguard trotted along beside her. *Good dog.*

Captain Lomax pressed Luke's shoulder. "Where does she think she's going? It's cold out there!" He grabbed Nantai's jacket from its peg, and shoved it into Luke's hands. "You seem to hold some sway. Get her back in here, Lieutenant. Women!"

As Luke suspected he would, Bodyguard led the beautiful Frenchwoman to where the Americans had pulled her plane from its cushion of evergreens. The dog stood by her now, as he often guarded a sheep lost from the flock.

Her flashlight clicked on, searched behind her. Luke stood still in the beam.

"Who is it?" she called out softly.

"Kayenta, Ma'am… Madame," he corrected, yanking his cap off his head.

Bodyguard trotted over and licked his hand.

"Only you?"

"Yes. And a coat. If you're cold."

He approached. She reached out for the garment. Her hand was as white as the moon, with long fingers, their nails painted the same lustrous red of her mouth. Luke slipped the sleeves over her arms, as if she were one of his nephews. The coat covered some of the crimson stains on her khaki trousers.

"My husband, he will recover?" she asked.

"Our medic thinks so, yes."

Her fragile smile strengthened. She threw her head back. "He is very handsome. When he heals, when the swelling goes down, you will see what a good choice I made. And Alain, he knows good hands. That is why he asked for your assistance, *Ange Lumiere*. He knows how useless I am when he is in egernace…emergence…how is it said? Sorry, I do not know the English."

Luke ventured closer. "Emergency?"

"Yes, so. Emergency," she sounded out carefully. "Only for that man am I this way, you understand. I have wonderful calm in the service of others. All but him, you see?"

"There was great use in what you did to calm us all with your song, I think. And you sing much better than the men recite poetry."

"Is that what their babble was? Poetry?"

"Well, rhymes."

76

She laughed. The sound went brittle, then wild. Her eyes filled with tears. Had he said something wrong?

"*Mon Dieu*, my hands—" she cried, holding them before her as if they didn't belong to her. Their shaking traveled up her arms to her shoulders.

"Here. Put them here," Luke urged, opening his coat. He felt them; cold, trembling, as she dug through the layers of his clothing, against his ribs, scratching him in her panic. He found a chant inside him. He sang it for Isabelle Marius and the juniper bushes, for they brought the plane down with its life and courage intact. He sang the end in English, improvising extra notes to make the language fit.

Now the woman,
With the rainbow,
Her treasure makes her holy,
With it she is encircled.
Happily she recovers.
Happily her interior warms.
Happily she goes forth.

She lifted her head. Her hair was the color of night, like that of the other airman's wife.

"The shaking," she whispered, "it is our secret, yes?"

"What shaking?"

She smiled that dazzling smile that this time was for him alone.

"Your woman is very lucky, Lieutenant."

He grunted. "Yes. She's never seen me."

"Oh? And why is this?"

He shrugged. Why had he told her this? He did not wish her to know the peculiar nature of his heartsickness. "She...lives in a different world," he tried.

Her laugh again, like bells now. "Ah, my angel, there is but one world, one life. We must cherish it and those we love, for we are only valued by the others for the things we carry."

Yes, they understood each other, Luke thought. She carried papers; he carried the coded form of his language in his head. What was it Mr. Spenser said that he and Nantai would become? If they worked hard devising the code, if they became strong in sending, in receiving, they would become walking, talking code machines. Machines. Valued for what they carried. He breathed in the frosty air of the small space between him and Isabelle Marius, and her sadness became his own.

Her finger stroked down the side of his face. "Your woman is beyond your reach? *Quel dommage*. But nothing is so certain as change, yes? What is your Christian name, Lieutenant?"

"Luke."

A smile of pure delight lit her face, erased all worry. "Ah. *Mais bien sur, bien!*"

"Ma'am?"

"I knew your name already, did I not? Luke is Lucius—light! *Ange Lumière*, my angel of light." She laughed, lighter, stones skimming water this time. It pleased him more than anything had in months, being the source of a woman's laughter.

"Hey, ya!"

Through the darkness, Nantai called, approached them on a run. Bodyguard answered with a bark of recognition.

"Come in, quickly, missus," Nantai told Madame Marius, with none of his usual reticence. "There is someone on the radio, calling for you!"

* * *

Inside Nantai's quarters, Luke stood breathless from their run as Isabelle Marius adjusted the headset over the waves of her dense black hair. She listened to the communication, and then replied in rapid-fire French. Luke saw a flash of her red nails before she took his sleeve. He stooped beside her.

She looked past him to where Captain Lomax stood. "A replacement plane, sir. I will guide the pilot in from here if your men will cast a net of light to aid his descent."

Captain Lomax nodded curtly. "Lieutenant Kayenta, you're on it," he said. "Take who and what you need."

Isabelle released him to his task.

Nantai held up flashlights. "To cover the four corners?" he asked.

"Yes. Two men on each," Luke directed, nodding toward Havlish and Ashton.

Back on the makeshift airfield, they were all still running for their stations when the sound of the aircraft reached Luke's ears.

"Switch on!" he called out.

Their lights streaked the sky.

The OSS man called Havlish let out a whoop. "Hey, it's an old FF1 — my brother trained on one of those. Fifi's a great old girl, and rugged! If anything can land on a dime, she can!"

"Keep the lights moving," Luke instructed, hoping Havlish was right about the small aircraft.

It circled the high valley twice, sounding strong, bearing itself steady. But Luke sensed something wrong. Deep pain. Listen, he sent out a message to the pilot, listen to the woman guiding you. He imagined Isabelle's calm, low tones, like a mother urging her little one to take his first steps. Listen.

The plane approached, made a smooth descent until a sudden gust rocked it. Near to where Isabelle had come down, but at a slower speed. It bumped back into the air, but landed about twenty feet short of the juniper bushes.

The guiding men's jubilation sobered as they drew closer.

The biplane had taken gunfire. The retractable canopy over its single cockpit opened. Luke saw a hand grip the side. Then it seemed to lose its strength. The men hushed. Nantai backed away from the dangling hand.

Luke climbed up on the lower wing.

He saw the top of a man's capped head, a larger, leather version of a sheepskin hat that was how the women at home kept their babies' ears warm in winter. Slowly, the pilot lifted his head. Luke recognized him at once.

Philippe Charente.

"Good evening," he said. "Would you kindly tell Madame Marius to pack up her husband and her bottles of *Je Reviens perfume*? Her chauffeur is here."

Before Luke could answer, Corbett reached into the cockpit.

"Shit. Oh, shit," he whispered. "Keep him talking, conscious. I'll be right back." He looked over his shoulder. "And don't let her in there."

But Isabelle Marius was already at the plane.

Chapter 7

Luke's hands circled the small waist to steady her as Isabelle Marius reached into the cockpit.

"Philippe, what have you done?" she demanded.

"You look very beautiful tonight, Madame Marius."

She flashed a sudden, bright smile at the compliment. "But of course — our *ange lumière* has wrapped me in the rainbow of his poetry."

He smiled like a drunken man. "I see it."

The pilot's head dropped back as a small groan escaped him. "Fifi is not nearly so damaged as I am. She will get you and Alain and the papers to London."

"And you."

The wounded airman lifted his head higher, scrutinizing Luke more closely.

"Ah, *Les Américaine Indienne*. It is said that you and your *petit cousin* are doing your work well here."

Keep him talking, Corbett had instructed.

"Is your wife well, Captain?" Luke blurted out. "You showed us many photographs of her, while we were in training, remember?"

Isabelle's long nails grazed Luke's back lightly. "And our Lieutenant *Lumière* does not forget a beautiful woman."

The pilot nodded. "My wife writes of her good health, thank you. And do you know, a child is coming with the summer? Can you imagine me a father, Isabelle?"

"*Mais bien sur!* Exactly what you need, to settle you. Your Kitty is most clever."

"I hope for a daughter. With the eyes and good sense of her mother. Her father has none at all, I fear."

His last word turned into a deep groan.

Flinging his satchel at Isabelle, Corbett rejoined them. The medic handed Luke a rubber tube. "Slip off his coat. Easy. Then pull this tight there— above the elbow," he directed.

With Captain Charente's arm exposed, the medic plunged the hypodermic needle into a vein.

The suffering in those sky-colored eyes began to ease. Their blue took on a glassy sheen. "Sheep," the airman whispered. "I smell sheep. Is this a farm?"

"One of two herding stations, sir," Luke told him. "Our small flock grazes at this higher altitude by day, then sleep down lower, at my station each night."

The airman's eyes scanned the hills silhouetted in the moonlight. "A good place. Like my Aunt Flore's farm in Quebec, near St. Jovite, in the Laurentian mountains. With sheep, and sugaring the maple trees in spring. I promised Kitty I would take her there when her French was better. You will take her there for me, perhaps, Lieutenant?"

"I do not speak French, sir."

"No matter. You can tap the maple from the trees, yes? In the spring? Being of the first people, the people who taught us French immigrants how to do it? You can teach this to my city girl, to my little daughter?"

"I am not from the northland. There are no maples where I come from, Captain. The Navajo are a desert people."

The airman snorted a short laugh. "Listen, Isabelle. Listen how gracious and mature I am becoming as he protests too much. I'm not challenging with a duel to the death this man who is in love with my wife!"

"Très bien, cherie," she whispered.

The airman's hand reached Luke's shoulder, drew him close. "Isabelle and Alain, into the air before dawn, you understand? There is no other hope for them or their mission."

He loosened his hold. "Now, Lieutenant *Lumiere*, as well as I feel now, I think I am still gunned to pieces. Perhaps you would be kind enough to help me to the ground?"

* * *

Isabelle Marius, true to her word, provided excellent, calm assistance to their medic. Once inside, her husband gave up his bed by the fire and helped settle the new patient in.

Bodyguard chose Luke's company as he approached the resting Ashton and Corbett outside Nantai's small shelter. The men looked like children to Luke, sleeping as if they had years of tomorrows. Lander and Yuli stood by them, on guard.

Alain Marius, flanked by Havlish and Isabelle sipped coffee.

Just as he was wondering where his clanbrother was, Nantai emerged from his escape hatch door and sat noiselessly beside Luke.

"Is he—?" Luke asked.

"No, but the medic does not know how he still breathes. His pain will be very great if the morphine runs out. Listen, my brother. These people don't know our ways. They don't know that we should not be with him, after."

Luke frowned. "We are soldiers."

"We are Dinè first."

"Yes. With relatives who will sponsor a ceremony, who will engage a Singer and a Medicine Person to help us find balance again. After our time as soldiers."

Captain Lomax ducked through the front doorway and joined them. "Your rank makes you gentlemen second in command of our new, expanded band. I just received our latest transmission from the radio. Let's consult on our next course of action, shall we?"

Luke looked, puzzled, at Nantai. A *belegaana* doing anything but issuing orders was unusual. Their attention soon returned to the officer as all the soldiers gathered around them.

Captain Lomax looked into each man's eyes before he began. This was not rudeness here, in the American service, Luke reminded himself. It was something he and Nantai learned was expected, back in their first training days in San Diego. But he could see from Nantai's frown that his brother had forgotten the differences of custom.

"Gentlemen," Lomax began, "We've camouflaged the damaged plane. Our Free French have been cleared for take-off within the hour in their replacement aircraft. We remain here. Suggestions?"

Luke considered. "A move, sir," he began. "To my station at the lower altitude, for now. If we have been informed upon, and any of the local authorities come, they will come here, where the planes landed, I think."

"We can't move Captain Charente."

"I will stay, watch over him, sir," Luke offered.

"No," Corbett protested, "I'm medical officer, I should—"

"You are medic of our mission, soldier," the Captain reminded him. "I can't spare you, even for this. We are scheduled for rendezvous at San Sebastien harbor. With our escaped prisoners. As Kayenta and Riggs's work here has now been severely compromised, the powers that be say they're now part of our mission. And they will evacuate from the harbor with us. Lieutenant Kayenta, what do you think we are up against since this interesting new wrinkle dropped from the sky?"

Luke said the words as they came to him. "The local police force. And they might draw extra men from among the prison guards. Those guards have been hunting the Basque rebels and republicans for years, they know this land well. Travel around them, and there will be fewer at the prison. I think you must free your captives soon, sir, for any chance of success."

"Travel now? In the dead of the night?"

"We have been mapping many paths to the prison on Mr. Spencer's orders, to prepare for your arrival. My clan brother will get you there in the dark."

They waited respectfully as their leader considered, reminding Luke of a council fire at home. Captain Lomax raised his head. "According to the transmission from our ship on the Atlantic, our shore transport boats are placed by local friends of San Sebastian, and the sea should be calm. You're right. We can't hesitate." He turned to Luke. "I could use your help, Lieutenant. In fact, I'm afraid I insist upon it. We will set up time for our radio connection. You will join us after that. If Captain Charante has not left us by then, I'm afraid you'll have to leave him."

The look in his superior's eyes reminded Luke of Jack Spencer's when they stood on the airstrip at the edge of America. Confidence and trust wrapped around the acceptance that most of what would happen was out of their hands. He smiled.

"I'll make every effort to join you, sir."

"See that you do. From the looks of you, I'd hazard a guess that you're not a favorite among the locals around here."

"Oh the locals and I get along fine, sir. It was a couple of tourists I displeased. German tourists."

"Hellfire," the captain breathed out. "We need to get you guys out of here."

* * *

Nantai grabbed Luke's sleeve as they left the meeting. "We did not talk it over, decide together who would stay behind. You are the better shot!"

"And you're the better tracker."

"You would not get them lost."

"Stop arguing. It does not look right."

"Because we are 'good' Indians? Missionary-tamed Indians?"

"Stop it, Nantai."

"I am allowed to argue with you. We hold the same rank."

"The time for arguing is finished. We have our orders."

Nantai's look darkened. "That is only because you can talk to them better, College Boy."

"And isn't that your luck?"

No. Stupid thing to say. Luke wished he could pull back the words. He walked faster. They must not fight. They must think of the good of the others.

Nantai grabbed his arm, turned him. "Hear me. You will be on a death watch. What will happen once he's gone?"

"I will do everything in the right way."

"And burn the bed? The dwelling? It is where I slept, not you. The *chindi*—"

"This place is full of what is left of the neglected dead! Can't you feel them?"

Luke closed his eyes. He had been rude, twice interrupting, like a *belegaana*. "Ashkii Dighin," Luke said his clan brother's sacred name softly, "we do not have the choices we have at home. But neither do these people with us. The Americans would rather be sleeping in their own beds, I think. And these French would like to have a homeland again. Captain Charente did not invite the wounds that will widow his wife, orphan his child. We are all of us soldiers, my brother. Soldiers first. It has to be so."

Silence remained between them until Nantai raised his head.

"The east. Remember to carry him out the eastern door."

"I know. I am Dinè."

"Huh. Too much inside school has not ruined your sense of direction, biologist?"

"I have some sense left, Desert Rat wrangler."

"College Boy."

Luke grinned, wanting to shove him like when they tussled in the new snow as children. But his clan brother held his arm now.

"When I watched the story of the monster climbing the needle building, the one in New York?"

"King Kong?"

"Yes. How I wish you had come with me, my brother. It was so exciting, But I did not think of the men in the flying aeroplanes, the ones that were trying to bring the monster down? Except in anger. Because I wanted the story to go on, you see? I did not want it to end yet. And now, these French people come in the same kind of aeroplanes. And this man, he will die, trying to keep evil from the world, from invading our home land. I was not thinking in the right way, when I watched King Kong. But you are doing the right thing, for the pilot."

All anger was gone from Nantai's face, replaced by deep sorrow.

"What will I tell your sisters?" he asked quietly. "I promised them I would look after you."

"Why did you do that?"

"They threatened me." He frowned deeply. "With castration."

Luke breathed out a sigh that turned into a laugh. "We are not alone here, my friend."

"True enough. There are all the *chindi*."

"And the *yeii*."

Nantai frowned. "*Yeii?* There are no holy ones to guide us in this place."

"There are, I think. Father Mikolas, in town. He lives in a sacred place, full of water spirits and deep peace. He stood up to the German soldiers, my brother, with only the fire in his heart. I think he must be guided by *yeii*. It would have made you sing, to see his courage. And he passed on the names of the ones to be freed from their suffering, names written into the Christian bread." Remembering the priest's instructions, Luke reached in his shirt pocket for the wrapped host. "He told me to give you some of this."

"Did he know we are not of his ways?"

"That would not be important to him, as it would not be with one of our holy ones."

The wrapping fell away. Nantai stared at what was left of the sacred bread. "You ate this?"

"Yes." Luke smiled. "And I still breathe."

Nantai shoved the battered and broken remains of the Eucharist into his mouth. He chewed, swallowed.

"Dry," he pronounced. "Wheat. No corn."

Luke cuffed the side of his clan brother's head. The playful gesture turned into what he hoped it would, an embrace.

"Stay well and join us," Nantai whispered into his shoulder, "I have no luck with the women, this we both know. But, still, I do not think I could live without my manhood."

"Don't worry. My sisters would curse your manhood away with their eyes long before they think to sharpen their knives."

Chapter 8

"So quiet."

The voice came through his light sleep. Luke lifted his head. He leaned forward. On Nantai's bed, the dog Bodyguard shifted, lending the airman more of his warmth.

"They have gone?"

"Yes, sir."

"Isabelle, Maruis…"

"Yes, sir. A good take off. Over the mountains."

"But left me the angel. And this marvelous creature here under my hand."

Luke smiled. "Yes. Bodyguard, too. And two more sheepdogs guarding the door."

"And the rainbow."

"Sir?"

"The colors. Around the one in the doorway. The one with the basket of bread."

Luke turned, hoping Nantai hadn't disobeyed orders and doubled back. But no one was there.

The pilot shifted his glance to the radio. "Any word? Of our fliers?"

"Yes. The message came through when you were sleeping. They are in England, safe."

"Ah, good."

Luke saw the deep pain the man had not complained about. He began to prepare one of the injections Corbett left behind.

"No morphine. Not yet. First. Help me finish a letter to my wife?"

"Yes, of course."

"It's in the lining of my cap. Deliver it, will you? Yourself, so that it passes through no other hands, no prying eyes? No censors?"

"I will," Luke promised, having no idea how he could accomplish it. He found the folded onionskin paper inside the soft leather cap. There was writing already on it in a cool, steady handwriting. Not enough. The airman had more to say. Luke pushed away the remaining dread of deep taboo and climbed into Nantai's bed. Bodyguard shifted as he used his body to prop up the airman. Philippe Charente wrote his good-bye to the woman they both loved — he deeply and Luke foolishly.

He worked hard even as his hand shook, even as beads of sweat appeared on his brow.

As Captain Charente finished, a coughing fit seized him. The bandages around his middle darkened with a deep stain. He sprayed a stream of bright red blood across the page. Luke yanked a handkerchief from his pocket and put it against the captain's mouth.

"*Dieu*, do not let her see that," he whispered.

"I'll clean it."

"But the words…"

"I will retrace them."

"Watch over her."

"Sir?"

"Spencer's front office. At the switchboard. You'll find her there. Do not let Jack stop you. Do not let anything stop you, my friend. The voices. They said I can hold the baby. They said I'll feel my legs again soon. Is this the truth?"

"Yes," Luke said, without thinking.

The airman rose a little on his own.

"The bread smells delicious," he said toward the empty doorway, with his last breath.

What fell back into Luke's arms felt lighter. He looked down as a breeze animated the dark waves of the airman's hair, worn longer than the American soldiers wore theirs, he realized, his thoughts splintering, spiraling, turning into whirlwind spirits, feeding off his fear.

He released the pilot and bolted from the bed, not stopping until he hit his shin against Nantai's small wash table. *Stop it. Return. Honor this man.*

What man? The wasp voices of the whirlwinds taunted him. *He's not here. You are alone.* Until they come for you too, with the rapid-fire guns that tore through Philippe Charante.

Luke forced himself to relax his shoulders, his arms. Slowly, he made himself look behind him.

The airman's eyes were still open. Bodyguard was still beside the dead man on the bed. Not making a sound. Looking at Luke with those soft dog eyes. Waiting patiently for the man he was to return.

What was the *belegaana* custom? He'd read about one in an old book. To close dead eyes with copper coins, payment for the boatman on a journey. He'd read good stories about the boatman, and the below world with a three-headed dog guarding it. The Dinè had below worlds too, so he felt connected to those stories.

Bodyguard whimpered, and finally left the bed. He trotted over and brushed his fur against Luke's leg, his shaking hand. Outside, Yuli and Lander called their greeting barks. Bodyguard returned them and soon all three dogs circled around him.

There was life still here in this place. To protect. And to keep him company. Bodyguard, Lander, Yuli, good and loyal four leggeds. *Think. Think of what to do.*

He walked back to the bed, made his shaking thumb find the Canadian's eyelids, close them. There, with the gesture, his own deep breathing returned. He prayed to know what to do next.

The simple rug Nantai had brought from home led the way for the airman's spirit to travel, out the sacred eastern door. Luke looked deeply into its arrow design. It was already accomplished, he realized. The airman was on his way.

Luke rose from the bed and began to prepare the body for burial.

Chapter 9

Bodyguard dragged his tools on a travois — a pick to break up the cold ground, and shovels. More than their weight slowed the dog's usual lively gait. Did he sense the sorrow of their task? Luke carried the airman's remains, wrapped in Nantai's rug. The burdened climb had Luke's muscles warmed for the labor of digging the grave.

Lander and Yuli guarded Nantai's camp. And down further, at Luke's camp, he pictured Nantai letting the sheep out of their corral. Would Luke hear their bells soon as they walked up to graze?

Peace infused the place where the mountain and sky met. A good place. Luke set down the wrapped body beside the pine tree and began to dig. The ground was hard, but not impossible to break apart.

He wished he knew a song for a burial, but his people had none. Others took care of the Dinè's dead, as they were forbidden to. From what spring had that taboo come? His grandmother thought it was from the time of the Long Walk and the exile in New Mexico, when disease had carried so many Dinè out of their lives.

He was a poor choice to be doing this. The airman deserved one of his own. *Never mind.* Keep digging, he told himself, deep enough that the remains will not be disturbed.

He had to step into the hole he was making. Fear stung at the root of his hair. He could only see a few stars. *Stop it. Keep digging. And think ahead.* When he and Nantai were gone, who would care for their sheep and their dogs? Surely Father Mikolas would send someone to bring them down off the mountain. Manchego will welcome them into his flock with their guardians, surely, and his daughter will weave their wool into fine rugs.

Almost done. He climbed back out, stood with his burden, holding his watch cap between his hands.

Luke remembered the spirit songs of a chain gang of prison workers he'd passed on the streets of Flagstaff once. One was a beautiful, tormented chant, looking for a long-gone mother, father, sister, brother. But a song that ended in light. Luke had tried to replicate the music on his flute. He heard the song in his mind now. The wind answered, whipping around him, swaddling the body of the airman tighter in his parachute. Deep peace filled Luke, assuring him that what he was doing was acceptable to the Spirits.

Luke faced the one who had been Philippe Charente. Squarely, not out of a corner of his sight as he had been doing since the man's last breath.

He needed to finish this. He was a soldier now. Perhaps this would be the first of many he'd be called upon to bury.

The airman was compact, like Nantai, like most of his own people. Not much trouble, even in death. Luke lowered the body into its snug spot in the earth.

He knew some prayers the Christian missionaries drummed into him so many years ago. But they were full of fear, of damnation and punishments. They did not seem right for this place, this occasion, this man, who had laughed so much back on that Atlantic crossing, and over the course of his training in England. Philippe Charente was of Canada, the land of English Protestant and French Catholic. "The Two Solitudes," Captain Charente had called his countrymen. Like the Hopi and his own people, Luke decided. The Hopi and Dinè shared land too, but not graciously, always fighting over water, instead of religion.

His knees ached, the cold night invading his joints. But he couldn't begin shoveling the dirt. Not yet. He must say something. Make a ceremony. He spoke quietly, "Returning you to our Mother, sir."

Bodyguard cocked his head. Another gust of wind answered, making Luke feel less foolish for talking to the dead. Finish, the wind seemed to say. So he replaced his hat and picked up the shovel.

Did any part of Philippe Charente still live, Luke wondered as he worked. Beyond his good natured teasing, did the airman truly know the heart of the one he'd trusted with that letter to his wife?

There was deep love between the two. Perhaps the airman's wife would hate him, the messenger who could not keep her husband from dying. What would he do then, if she hated him?

He was thinking much too far ahead. And the chances that he himself would survive to visit the airman's wife were poor. Still, he would keep the promise, if he could.

Luke placed his tools on the travois. He and Bodyguard started for Nantai's home.

He turned back only once, when he reached a landmark — a boulder outcrop, shaped like a great turtle's back, which would be there no matter what happened to the land for years to come. Luke leaned on Turtle's back and looked up the moonlit hill where he'd buried the airman, setting the place in his heart.

The grave was lonely, solitary, like Luke felt at this moment.

He and the airman, the two solitudes.

He had one more task — the Dinè obligation he'd promised Nantai he would perform, before he went on to find his clan brother and the Americans.

Nantai built his place in the mountains like a hogan, because Nantai had never lived with the *belegaana*, and had never been a Christian.

His parents had hid Nantai every Fall, when the missionaries came to gather up the children for boarding school. It was Luke who had taught his friend English, learning it better himself, forgetting less over the summers home because his friend was so eager, such a good scholar.

Soon Nantai's place reeked with the kerosene he'd used on the bedding, the blankets, the simple wooden furniture. Luke struck a match, flung it inside, and turned away.

The small structure of logs, mud, and brush did not take long to burn. The fire never jumped out of the ring of dirt he'd dug around it. Still, Luke stood guard, the shovel in his hands.

Bodyguard joined the two other dogs in a forlorn whine.

Luke checked his weapons. He wound his grandfather's watch. It was almost the appointed time for his scheduled contact with the rest of their new mission, their final mission in Spain. He charged the radio, strung the aerial. He found the frequency, sent out the contact code.

Instead of Nantai's answer, he heard words in Spanish-accented English.

"Señor Kayenta. We have your friends. We will kill them, one at a time, unless you join us here."

"It's a lie! They don't have us all —" a voice broke in.

A gunshot followed echoed across the high valley, from his sheep station.

"That's one," the first voice said.

The transmission ended.

Stunned, Luke stared at the box sticking out of its concealment within Nantai's portable gramophone.

He ripped off the earphones, threw back his head and lifted his voice in a war chant.

* * *

Kitty Charente knew something was wrong. Deeply wrong.

It wasn't the flowers. Or, rather, lack of them. Every week since Philippe left, Jack came to work with bigger and bigger bouquets---lilies, roses, great shoots of gladiolas. How had he found them in the depths of winter, she'd wondered. The rich knew how to get a hold of anything, so her sister Anna said, but not too disdainfully, as the flowers passed on to her own apartment once they'd crowded out Kitty's place.

But today Jack himself stood before her switchboard, rumpled, his eyes swollen, his homburg hat between his hands. Forgetting his weekly bouquet. Forgetting even to greet her.

"Come into the office, Kitty," he said.

She followed him, her knees buckling a little, knowing. Knowing, but telling herself it was the new shoes, the ones she shouldn't have bought last payday. She was going to be someone's mother, she had to stop buying shoes on a whim.

He made her sit, not at her dictation chair beside his desk, but on the long, elegant sofa that dominated the opposite wall. He sat on the ottoman across from her, forearms resting on his knees.

"He went down."

Her heart twisted, and then calmed, an unnatural calm.

"Where?"

"I can't tell you that, Kitty."

"Not the water. Please, Jack. Not the water." She couldn't bear to think of him, who so loved the clouds, ending up in the cold depths of the sea.

"No," he confirmed. "Not the water."

Then she closed her eyes. And saw it all.

"He was shot down."

He flinched. "Who told you?"

"You. You're telling me."

"No, you are telling me."

She shrugged, suddenly feeling very tired. "Ask Mama, she can explain it. Family trait. 'The knowing,' she calls it. One of those old country things. Passed down. And useless. It's not like we can change anything, is it?"

"Kitty—"

"Last night I dreamed he was holding the baby. At the foot of our bed he stood, smiling, lost in her. A girl, just the baby he wanted. When I woke up, I felt so alone without them."

She'd felt that way since they'd said their good-byes in that borrowed car on the Long Island airstrip, she realized now, her fingers tingling, her toes cold and stiff in her new shoes.

Find your breath, she told herself. Talk. "He had something around his waist," she babbled, "bright red, a sash really, like his grandfather's French Canadian Voyager belt. In my dream, I mean. Is that where their guns hit him?"

"I...I don't know." He cleared his throat. "It was quick, he didn't suffer."

"You don't know where he was hit, but you know that?"

Had lies always followed Jack's throat clearing, Kitty wondered. She had to listen more carefully for that trait from now on, she told herself. "I want to hold him," she demanded now, "when is he coming home?"

"They can't risk it. Kitty. He saved lives. And vital information. We have to be content with that."

"Why? If he's dead, why can't I have him?"

The words ended in a wail. The sound she made reminding Kitty of her mother, when she learned that her brother, the brakeman, had been crushed between two railroad cars. Then she was standing, ready to run, ready to escape this turn her life had taken. Jack wrapped his arms around her. He held something to her lips. Brandy. "Please, Kitty," he whispered, "Just a sip."

She obeyed, welcoming the heat it brought to her insides. He lifted her in his arms like a child and brought her back to the sofa, then blanketed her with his jacket before resuming his place on the ottoman.

There, he stared down at his hands.

When their eyes met again there were tears in his. He was a feeling man, for all his easy banter, and the way he skimmed surfaces of care, like most of the rich. A feeling man, who'd suffered his own losses.

"I'm sorry, Kitty," he whispered. "I'm so sorry."

"I am too. For you, I mean. You knew him longer. Philippe said you warned him away from me at first. It's true, isn't it?"

"Yes."

"Not because of what my sister Anna thinks—that I wasn't a good catch — not rich, or educated past high school. Not because I wasn't good enough for your friend."

"Of course not."

"Because of this. Because this was a possibility. An odds-on possibility."

"Yes. Gus is picking up your mother, your sister. They'll be here soon to take you home. You know you don't have to worry about anything, don't you, Kitty?"

"Don't fire me. Please, not yet. Not until the baby's born."

"We can talk about that—"

"Now, please. Let's talk about that. About anything, Jack."

She caught a whiff of his cologne. Her brothers had made fun of Jack Spencer, way back. She was so young when she started at the factory that they came to pick her up from work after dark. That's when they met her boss, who

104

spent too much money on his clothes in the middle of a depression and wore scent. Now his sandalwood was tinged with the salt of his sweat. He'd lost his young wife to the Spanish Flu. Philippe told her that.

"Tell me how you did, Jack."

"Did?" he prompted.

"Went on. After you lost her."

She had his hand, he couldn't get away, not honorably. And Jack Spencer was an honorable man. His head dropped forward.

"You won't learn anything useful from me, little one," he whispered.

Chapter 10

Luke ran. He ran harder than at festival times at home. The dogs stayed with him, Bodyguard in front, Lander and Yuli at his right and left flank.

How had Captain Lomax's men been caught? Their captors must have circled around, surrounded them. He should have left one or two of the dogs with Nantai and Captain Lomax and his men. They would have provided warning. Luke thought of the brave voice, interrupting, silenced with a shot. Which of the men had spoken? Was he dead? *Don't think of the faces, the lopsided grins.*

A full capture was a lie, the voice had said over the radio. So, others of the band were still free? How many? Were they armed? Where were they?

Bodyguard stopped, growled.

The other two dogs stood in front of Luke, preventing him from advancing.

A quiet voice sounded from above. "Lieutenant?"

Luke looked up, scanning the pine's branches. Ashton and Corbett's faces appeared. They climbed down. Bodyguard earned a head rub of thanks.

"Don't go to your place by yourself, sir," Private Ashton said.

"I'm glad I won't have to. All the rest are there?"

"Yes, sir."

"What happened?"

"Ambushed, near as we can figure." the medic replied. "We were running behind on account of us stopping so I could wrap Ashton's foot tighter. When we came to the last bend up there, we saw Captain Lomax and the boys rounded up, under guns, sir. Then, some rough Spic— Spanish— Spanish talk."

The two men looked at each other.

"Go on," Luke said.

"Well," Ashton took up the story. "At first Lieutenant Riggs was giving a good cover story in Spanish to them, near as I can tell. So we're thinking okay, so far so good, you know? But I guess they quit buying it."

"When?"

"Well, when they smacked him around pretty good, sir."

Luke felt an ache at his jaw.

"But they shoved him back with the rest of the guys, after."

"I see"

Corbett frowned hard. "I'm sorry, lieutenant. It wasn't supposed to be like this. We weren't supposed to interfere, blow your cover identities."

"My partner will be all right." Luke tried to clear the gruffness from his voice. He needed to think. Of a plan for the rescue of the rescuers. "What weapons do we have?"

"Me? I was issued a silenced Sten, the medical equipment, and the money belt."

"Ashton?" Luke inquired, hoping his mounting desperation wasn't seeping through his tone.

"I've got a Welrod, sir, also silenced."

"Sighted?"

"Sergeant Havlish has the sight, sir. Sorry."

"It is enough," Luke decided. "We'll get them out."

With a barely armed medic and a limping man, Luke finished his own outlandish statement in his head, but had the sense not to voice it. *Or die trying.* "How's the leg, Ashton?" he asked instead.

"I got up the tree and away from your dog's teeth fast enough on it, sir."

"That's good." Luke turned to Corbett. "Who has our men? How many?"

"I counted twelve guys, sir. Four in the prison guard uniforms — we were briefed on how they'd look, and four local police, I think."

"And the last four?" Luke prompted. He didn't like it when these men hesitated. Worse news always followed.

Corbett took in an uneven breath. "Germans."

"Germans?"

"I think so. In fancy mountain-climbing civvies, of course. Maybe your two bully boys among them, you think? We were briefed to be watchful for them, the Germans. They're on

108

leave, relaxing here, right? But, you know what? They brought machine guns on vacation."

Had they seen him wince at the thought of taking on seasoned German soldiers with machine guns? *Say something. Make up for it.* He was now their commanding officer. "Well," he tried, "could be worse."

Ashton grinned. "Sure, lieutenant. A couple of vacationing Mussolini's boys might a happened by too."

"Maybe *Il Duce* himself. Bet he's a fair shot," Corbett contributed.

"And what kind of shot are you?" Luke asked.

The medic sobered, pulling on his earlobe. "Truth to tell, I'm better at finding a vein, sir."

"Here." Luke pulled out two Colt .38 Supers from his rucksack and placed one in each man's hand. "We will have to surprise them, make them think we're a bigger force than we are. Use your silenced weapons first, they won't realize they are under attack. Then the other weapons, after they know what is happening. Remember your training. Kills are to head or heart, but not easy targets. To stop someone, mid-body will do. One weapon in each hand, each of them ready. Do you understand?"

"Yes, sir," they answered together.

"They shot Havlish, sir," Ashton whispered.

It was Sergeant Havlish, then, who was the brave one, the one who spoke up. Luke nodded. "Dead?"

"I can't be sure, sir."

"Maybe he'll help us, then, if he can. Along with the others. After we get them out of range of those machine guns. That is our job. Come. I'll show you where to take cover."

Ashton took his arm. "Lieutenant, what's your weapon?"

"A flashlight."

"A flashlight?"

"Modified by the OSS. Don't worry about me. It will defend me. And do some damage, if my aim is true."

"Oh."

"They radioed that they want me. Alive, I think, at least for now. They're waiting for me. I can't appear with you two, or seem to be armed. So I will walk in, hands raised, with the dogs. While I talk, get your targets in range. When the dogs leave my side— that is the signal to move forward. Fire your silenced weapons first, then, with everything you have. Remember, take on the machine guns first."

They nodded.

"Good, then. Let's move."

Corbett stood his ground. "Sir? Do we have any chance against them?"

Luke grinned. "I don't know. The dogs have good sharp teeth. Can you two fight better than you recite poetry?"

"Much better," they assured him, almost in unison.

As they took cover on the outskirts of his now-crowded camp, Luke took stock of the situation. The system he often saw at work among the *belegaana* was in place. Two Germans watched the two prison guards as they ordered the four local police to build up the campfire. First, second, third class. As in their army, and on their train and ship passage.

Four of the enemy were within his rough sheep station home, overseeing seven captives: two prison guards and two Germans. Just barely within, Luke guessed, from the single oil lamp's light at the window, from the darkness on the second floor. Inside, Nantai was hurt, Sergeant Havlish wounded or dead. Luke knew he had to get the two remaining German machine gunners out in the open, or they could lose all of the captives in a single burst of fire.

"Keep watch on the dogs," he reminded Ashton and Corbett.

They nodded.

Luke smiled at their young, open faces. He felt, for the first time in his life among white people, that he was not looking at strangers.

"You honor me," he told them.

Corbett swallowed hard. "Good luck, sir."

Luke's nostrils filled with crisp winter air, and he thanked the cougar who had appeared before him at another time, on another mountain, when he was fourteen. He called on the animal's spirit to visit him again. Then he sent the dogs away from his side, giving them their positions and the stay signal.

He took in a breath, whistled a signal he had taught them over their days of herding sheep together. Would they remember? Lander whined, Bodyguard growled, Yuli performed his best yipping, as if he'd found a mouse under the snow.

Good dogs.

Luke heard the bolt of a rifle. It belonged to a Spanish prison guard, the mustached one. "Who's there?" he called out from behind the banked campfire. "Stand!"

Luke obeyed, slowly lifting his hands in the air, and whistling another signal to the dogs. The dogs joined him, and took turns brushing their tails against his legs. These loyal, beautiful animals should not be here, Luke thought suddenly. They should be with the sheep.

"I am Kayenta the shepherd, *mi guardia*," he called out, keeping his Spanish slow and with a New World accent, without a lisp. "Perhaps you know me, from when I come down to the village for supplies. Sometimes you are in Manchego's cafe, yes? I heard gunfire and do not understand what is going on. Do you? Have you seen my partner?"

"It is not for you to question us," the mustached one pronounced. "What is it that you carry?"

"A light. See?" Luke flicked the switch of the flashlight, sending a beam into the shadows beyond the fire to the ones with the machine guns.

"He has only a torch," the local guard repeated to the Germans.

"Come closer," a German in a green tourist's hat said as he rose from his canvas chair. He addressed Luke directly, in English. "And control those animals, or you are a dead man."

"They are under control, sir."

As he approached, Luke kept his knees loose, flexible. Ready.

The Germans and the Spaniards positioned themselves in a half moon around the fire, facing Luke and the dogs. What could he do to get the other machine guns outside? The mustached prison guard stepped forward.

The German frowned and then gave a slight nod.

It should have been enough of a warning, but Luke was watching the German, thinking he would do his own dirty work. A mistake. He was forgetting their system, their class system.

His peripheral vision caught sight of the stock of a prison guard's rifle. Too late. One dog made a choice, without a signal, and leapt at his attacker.

Luke heard a shot as he ducked under the guard's swing. The blow only glanced off his cheek, but he stayed down, and still. He sensed a form crawl up beside him on the ground. He knew the dogs, had shared heat with all of them on the coldest winter nights.

This was the long, hairy coated one, who loved Bing Crosby. Bodyguard.

Luke felt himself descend under the fur, through layers of fine muscle, bone, heart. It was a good place to be, a place that had never known lies or cruelty, only joy in living, and loyalty.

His grandmother's skirts swished by, the familiar tinkling sound of the sheep bells in her wake. Her hand swooped through his hair. "Good, play possum," she said.

He blinked twice. Luke became aware of the other two dogs, restless, but staying by him, growling at the men, waiting for Luke's signal. Voices argued above him.

Another German soldier, a new one, from inside, with a machine gun strapped around his shoulder, was chastising the one who ordered the assault.

That one in turn, and in broken Spanish, was blaming the prison guard for knocking Luke unconscious.

Classes, more interested in their pecking order than in him for the moment. *Good.* One inside machine gun remaining. Luke shifted his view. There, yes. The last machine gun guard was standing in the doorway, watching the excitement. Lander and Yuli,'s snarls grew louder.

The green hat German noticed Luke's open eyes. "Ah, this is good," he said. "You are not rendered senseless at least, yes? We have gathered knowledge about you in the town. About both of Spencer's sheep men."

"*Agenten!*"

Luke knew that voice from the day before. Green Hat came closer. "You are not so bad,

114

yes, Spencer's man? Just a little play, that's what it was, outside the church!" he continued in gruff, almost jovial English.

Luke caught the scent of the apricot brandy that the people of Vincente gave as gifts. The more stern German smiled and placed his hand over his heart. "I apologize, Señor Kayenta, for your pain, from my brutish corporals, from these Spanish, who did a little damage to your fellow shepherd. He is well. You will see. Ach, it is so difficult to find good help in this country."

The smile disappeared.

He ordered something blunt, in German. Nantai's retrieval? No, the man must not get back inside with that deadly weapon. It was time to act.

Luke pulled the pin at the base of the flashlight. He tossed it into the night air as he signaled the dogs to attack.

Chapter 11

The guards cursed as Yuli and Lander dug teeth deep into their legs. The Germans, stunned, whipped their machine guns around. Silenced shots hit them mid-chest. A Spanish guard appeared at the doorway, just as the explosives hidden inside Luke's flashlight detonated, sending the banked fire flying in a hail of sparks and debris. And smoke. Luke rolled into the smoke as he dug for his Colt. He, Ashton and Corbett found cover.

"Stay down!" Corbett warned, opening fire. Enemy shots answered his. Luke hoped the medic was following his own advice as he watched the door, ready to shoot the next armed man to appear. Instead he heard a frantic call.

"*Alto! Nos rendimos!*" followed by American English. "Kayenta! Corbett! Ashton! Hold your fire! We've got the rest covered!" in Captain Lomax's voice.

Luke raised his hand to signal those under his command.

He stood in the smoking, wounded silence. Was it over? The world tilted, but his feet stayed flat on the ground.

The remaining guards came out of the dwelling, hands on their heads. Behind them, Captain Lomax and his men held guns on them. Havlish limped, nursing a crippled side. Not a fatal shot, then? Luke continued to count heads.

All there, except Nantai. Where was he?

A cloud of black blew in between him and the men. Luke lost his balance, somehow, and went to his knees. He smelled something dangerous, metallic. Was it the evil of those dead men that was swirling in his lungs?

He felt a firm grip at his shoulder, dragging him out of the whirlwind of the dead.

"Open your eyes, my brother."

Luke blinked twice, and saw Nantai and the medic Corbett. He focussed on his clan brother's

large sticking plaster, his bruises. "You look terrible," Luke told the one yanking him to his feet.

"Matching you, now," Nantai returned the compliment, his grin widening.

"How is Havlish?"

"Lucky. A graze...he has got a surface wound only."

Corbett peered over Nantai's shoulder.

"There are no other wounded, sir," he said quietly, without a hint of triumph in his voice. He was not a warrior, but trained to heal. "Guess we were better shots than we thought."

The medic's hands shook. They had just checked the dead men for pulses.

Behind him, Captain Lomax's men changed clothes with captives and the dead.

A rustling sounded. Feet, dropping down from trees, surrounding them. Where were the dogs, Luke wondered. Why weren't the dogs warning them? All went quiet as people of many shapes and sizes, surrounded them. All were armed, with pikes, daggers, an old hunting rifle or two. But their identities were hidden by hoods, kerchiefs, and swaths of embroidered scarves.

"Hands up, men," their captain quickly shouted.

Soldiers and Spanish prisoners alike did as commanded.

The masked people descended among them, pulling the bodies of the dead outside their circle and taking their prisoners under guard. And confiscating the weapons of their enemies, the Spanish and Germans. But they did not disarm any of the Americans.

A broad-chested man in black silk stepped forward.

"Senor Kayenta?" he asked in Spanish.

"Yes, sir?"

"For how long do these troublesome gnats need to be out of your way?"

"A day would serve us well, sir."

"It shall be done. And the dead ones they will never find. These mountains sometimes make people disappear. The gnats, if they desire to continue breathing, will report an unfortunate fall into a deep ravine took the lives of our German mountaineers."

"We are in your debt, sir."

"We hope to see your return in better times, sir. But for now, go with God."

As quickly as they had come, all disappeared back among the pines.

The men slowly lowered their arms in silence. "Friends of yours, gentlemen?" Captain Lomax asked.

"It appears so, sir," Luke answered. "But I don't know what we did to deserve them."

* * *

The medic shone a light in Luke's eyes.

"Good. They're dilating. Now, lean your head back so we can stop the bleeding."

"Bleeding?"

That metallic smell, and the wetness on his face. The rifle, of course, he remembered. He didn't quite get out of its way.

Nantai held his head steady as Corbett cleaned the wound. Luke felt a sudden ache of loneliness invade his bones.

"Where are Lander and Yuli?" he asked the medic.

Corbett continued his task. "Who?"

Luke looked to his clan brother, who suddenly found interest in the dirt on his coat. No, not his coat, another coat. When had he changed coats? "And Bodyguard. The dogs, Nantai. Where are the dogs?"

119

It was Corbett who answered. "None of them made it, sir. They took the hits for us. Too bad. Fine animals."

Luke felt a sting at his eyes. *Stop it.* They would not understand, and think him foolish.

There. Under control. Now think in the right way. Bodyguard had been true to his name. Lander and Yuli attacked his enemies on command, just as Corbett and Ashton had. They were loyal to their deaths. He thanked them. He promised to honor them in a song or a story.

Luke looked up to see Captain Lomax in one German's smart Tyrolean climbing suit. He fit into it well and replaced the dead man's light hair and eyes and broad features too. "Well, it looks like you have won the role of our prisoner, Lieutenant Kayenta. You'll be the only one of us not required to change clothes for the next phase of this operation."

The tallest three of Lomax's men wore the remaining Germans' clothes.

"Sure wish your Basque or hold-out republican friends had left us one of those machine guns," their captain said wistfully. But I suppose we should be happy we've still got our own weapons."

Nantai shifted uncomfortably in a bullet-riddled coat of a Spanish prison guard. Luke felt his friend's fear of the dead man's *chindi*. He wanted to say something, make a ceremony even, to help his clan brother stay in balance inside the clothes.

"Good thing it's dark," Captain Lomax said. "We'll only have to fool them long enough to reach the prison cells. Translations will be up to our Spanish speakers, Riggs, Ingrassia and Kayenta. Let's get out of here. We've got a rendezvous off the beach before the sun rises."

"What's our story, sir?" Ingrassia asked.

"Well, it goes like this; our two shepherds they proved themselves tough nuts to bring in for questioning. So our story going into the prison is this: you, Lieutenant Riggs, got clean away, so they should go looking, maybe send out a team right away, even, leaving fewer for us to deal with at the lockup, right? Next part of story: we managed to haul one of you in for them to help us interrogate. That would be you, Lieutenant Kayenta. We think you night be in league with American prisoners, that's why we need to haul their sorry asses out of their cells for questioning too."

He looked at Luke and shook his head. "By the way, you are both that."

"Sir?" Luke asked.

"Tough nuts. Thanks for taking what you took. Thanks for coming after us. We'll repay you in kind. It won't look like it, but we'll be following you into hell."

Chapter 12

The moon came out from behind a cloud. The prison loomed ahead, an ancient stone structure growing out of serene countryside.

Captain Lomax ordered Ingrassia to stop the car. Behind them, the truck followed suit and emptied. The men peered through binoculars.

"Porta Coeli, men."

"What does that mean?"

"Gate of Heaven," Luke translated. "It was a monastery, once."

"Looks like Luna Park at Coney Island," Private Ashton said

"Yeah, but darker," Frank offered. "These spoil sports turned off all the lights on the Electric Tower. And this place is bigger, isn't it?"

Captain Lomax grunted. "Not big enough to hold the men we came for."

"Naw, not that big," Sergeant Havlish took up his leader's signal. "Hell, Sing-Sing wouldn't be that big."

"Or Leavenworth," Corbett chimed in. "Not that I've ever been there, of course."

Luke looked toward Nantai and wondered if these Americans, so used to their freedoms, caught the scent of what he felt pulsing off the place. Or was their joking was a guard against it: that despair, centuries deep and imbedded in the night air?

"Well, our ship awaits. Let's relieve one of General Franco's monasteries turned into prisons of its crowded conditions," their captain commanded.

Luke was glad he was not Captain Lomax, the brash, smiling man with wheat-colored hair, who believed that everything was possible.

"Lieutenant Kayenta," he summoned, "help me figure something out. Who do you suppose sat where in these vehicles?"

Luke looked into the windows of the large car, thinking of the *belegaana* class system and catching the scent of hair pomade and cigar smoke. "The German leader and a driver here," he guessed. "The rest in the truck, maybe."

"Sounds right. Let's have our drivers do the talking. Ingrassia, exchange clothes with Mort, we'll need to make you one of the Spanish-speaking Germans."

Ingrassia gave a half smile. "Well, I'm coming up in the world."

Good plan, Luke thought, although he wished Nantai, their remaining Spanish speaker, had gotten the job, so they would be closer to each other.

"Lieutenant," Lomax told Luke, "we'll keep their attention on you as much as possible.

Ingrassia, you'll instruct the gatekeepers to make sure we've got the right man. As they're verifying his identity, do what you can to find out where our prisoners are."

"Right, Captain."

"Lieutenant Riggs," Lomax turned his attention to Nantai now, "I'm leaving the truck and the rest of my men in your hands. We're the scout vehicle. You're backup force and getaway. You and Sergeant Havlish will remain with the truck. Once we come back, do your level best to get us on the road to San Sebastian and that beach."

Cast in the middle of the larger team, Nantai looked out of place and alone. As Ashton, and Corbett took places in the back of the truck, Nantai climbed into the driver's seat beside his fellow disguised German, Sergeant Havlish. Luke walked over, stood on the running board, touching his clan brother's coat sleeve, so at least they would both share the contamination of the dead German.

"We can do this, Monster Slayer," he said quietly in Dinè.

"I don't have your smooth tongue."

"Well. We speak three languages. Most of them can't speak at all in this place."

"True enough."

Luke wanted to promise Nantai that they would ask their elders for an Enemyway ceremony soon, when they got home. But Captain Lomax was issuing more orders, so he gave his clan brother's forearm a quick squeeze.

"Well, my poets. Our theater of war awaits. God help us talented amateurs in our stage debut."

"Yes, sir!" they huffed their affirmation in unison.

Luke and Nantai were the outsiders, a step behind the squad's well-practiced rituals. Still, the men's gritty, soot-stained faces looked like relatives.

He took his station between Private Ingrassia and Captain Lomax.

The moonlit sky, now bright, cast shadows over the snow. It was quiet inside the big, well-cushioned automobile. The captain watched the road as he spoke. "Lieutenant Kayenta, if there was a way to keep you out of this, I would have taken it."

"I understand, sir."

He relaxed a little into the oiled leather seats of the automobile. "We're way off the game plan. There will be hell to pay with our bosses, no matter how this goes down. But that's part of the job, being good at improvisation."

They hit a hole in the road deep enough that Luke's head hit the ceiling, but it, too, was padded. The captain kept talking. "Your boss Spencer's a patrician... more like his pal the head man, isn't he?"

"Head man?"

"You know, that guy with the cigarette holder, who makes a good speech, but can't even control his own wife?"

"You mean President Roosevelt, sir?"

"I do. Wrists together, now."

He began to casually bind Luke's hands with leather. "Hmmm, you're barely in your twenties, aren't you? Roosevelt's the only president you remember?"

"Well, yes, sir."

"Do I sound disrespectful? FDR is bit of a 'great father' to you people, is he?"

Luke smiled with half his mouth. Among themselves, the Dinè had many names for American presidents, but 'great father' was not one of them. And Roosevelt's man Collier, he was the one who sent Bureau of Indian Affairs people to kill Navajo sheep and goats over the Great Livestock Massacre time. Luke could sometimes still hear their animals screaming in his dreams. But he came from warriors. And the homeland was attacked. He would do as his grandmother had advised. He would fight to protect the United States, their Mother.

He looked down at the leather bindings at his wrists. He knew they were necessary, but he hated the constriction. He could take beatings better than this, he realized. *Not good. Swallow it, swallow it. Listen.* Try to make sense of what his captain was saying. Lomax placed the slip knot between his thumb and forefinger, his way to quickly release himself, and kept talking.

"I suppose no man can help what he's born into, even Spencer and Roosevelt with their stiff jaws and blue blood ways. Even the communist Jews of the Lincoln Battalion we're set to spring from the prison. Thus Nazis and this war makes egalitarians of us all. Hell, one thing I know. Spencer may not look tough, but he picks men as tough as they come."

Between Captain Lomax's clipped speech and fighting his own mounting panic, Luke gave up trying to follow what his superior was talking about. The end of it sounded like a compliment, so he thanked him. But though he had the means to his own freedom under sweating fingers, he didn't feel nearly as tough as they come.

"All will be forgiven if we get our cargo on that ship that's waiting for us. And Lieutenant, it doesn't matter how or when you and Riggs came into our fold. We'll watch your backs."

"Thank you, sir."

The searchlight caught their vehicles in its glare. They slowed before the guardhouse that was built into the stone wall courtyard. Captain Lomax lowered his head, allowing only glimpses of his pale jaw and light hair. "Look more scared now," he counseled, "I'm one mean son of a bitch Nazi, even on vacation."

Luke heard Ingrassia demand confirmation that their captive was one of Spencer's shepherds. His Spanish was not like either Luke's or the locals, so perhaps it was strange enough to sound German-influenced.

A pause. Too long a pause. Luke's bowels clenched. Captain Lomax pulled Luke's head back by his hair.

"El pastor, el pastor!" Ingrassia shouted.

"Oh, to be sure, that's the shepherd!" the guard answered. "Excuse me for my hesitation, sir. His face is a little changed…which I'm sure he deserved." He punctuated his opinion with a spit aimed at his own boots.

"Where are the American prisoners held?" Ingrassia demanded next.

"The Americans? Under the tower, sir."

The guard was looking into the car more closely.

Luke tried to distract him. "This is a mistake! My superior Señor Spencer, he will pay. You would like some perfume for your woman?"

"Nein, nein, nein!" Captain Lomax shouted, punctuating each repetition with a slam of Luke's head into the dashboard. Not hard, so Luke slapped its underside with his bound hands to increase the effect.

The guard backed away, and Ingrassia turned the wheel toward the tower.

"Boatload of German phrases from my uncle Heimbert the butcher in Chicago, and all I can think of is '*nein*,' Lomax muttered. "Sorry, Lieutenant."

"That's all right, sir."

He looked to their driver. "Good work, Ingrassia. Double-time, now. You ready to bully those cell keys into our possession?"

"Ready, sir."

Ingrassia led, barking orders at sleepy night shift guards. He kept his demands for the keys simple; *"Llaves. Todos."* When three guards

128

tried to join them, he held up his hand. "Very secret. Remain here."

"As you wish," their leader replied. But his eyes widened as he saw the men jump down from the back of Nantai's truck. "Who are they? Shall I wake the commander?" he asked Lomax.

"No. Return to your duties." Ingrassia growled, walking faster, in boots that were too large for his feet.

As the crew descended the wide stairs under the tower, Luke yanked the slip-knot, freeing his hands from their leather restraints. The enveloping darkness cloaked them. So many steps, he lost count, deep in the earth that was carved and heavily fortified.

Finally, level floor. The bottom. Corridors shooting off from the Americans' section under the tower. Scars on the stone wall, speaking of fires, of floods, of violence. Luke fought the bile coming up his throat. He calmed himself with thoughts of Dinè creation stories, of his ancestors emerging from a place like this, deep in the earth, to begin life on fifth world, after all their tribulations among insect people, and bird people, the arguments between the men and the women, the battles between monsters and the holy. If his ancestors could survive, so could he. He almost laughed. He did not think he still believed those stories.

No sounds. Ancient wooden doors with the numbers burned in were strapped in iron. No bars, so nothing of the prisoners could be seen, not even their eyes. A good thing, Luke decided,

129

for if he could see the beings beyond those doors he would be tempted to free them all.

Ingrassia handed the keys to their captain, who opened the ring. Swiftly, silently, each man took the key that would unlock the name burned into his memory with a rhyme. Luke's obligation was to a small child who had been kind to him. He felt the embedded mark in the cold iron.

Thirty-eight.

He set off along a snaking path away from the tower and searched for the cell of Arturo Castile.

Chapter 13

Luke opened the cell door, breathing in the macabre atmosphere; humans, animals, sometimes fighting each other for survival, sometimes feeding off each other. And suffering, so much suffering.

Sift through it all, Luke commanded himself, as he flicked on his flashlight. Find him.

"Arturo Castile?" He called.

Nothing.

He heard breathing, turned his light in its direction, the corner, and, and a mound of filthy rags. No, not rags. A man.

"Señor Castile?"

"Who are you?"

"Someone your daughter was kind to. Would you like to leave?"

He looked over Luke's shoulder, where Ingrassia stood with his own freed charge, and spat. "Not with Germans."

"They're only German coats."

"Prove it."

Mort joined Ingrassia and shoved Luke's shoulder. "Hey, Lieutenant, better get going. It's the bottom of the ninth here."

The prisoner shook his head, and switched his language to English. "Never mind," he said, climbing to his feet. "No people mangle language like Americans."

Luke marveled at the quiet efficiency of the men as they moved the liberated prisoners up the dim, winding steps back to the surface. Not as ill-used as Arturo Castile, they kept in step. Ingrassia, in his German coat, stayed in the lead. He did not stop until challenged.

"Por favor—"

Ingrassia turned, stared the prison guard down. But when the guard meekly asked what was going on, and why they have local prisoners in custody, Ingrassia's jaw tensed.

Luke found the Spanish to beg forgiveness of Arturo Castile for naming him a co-conspirator with the American escape plan. Castile caught on and had the good sense to spit in Luke's face.

Ingrassia laughed. "Soft American. Didn't take him long to betray, did it?" he asked the guard.

"But, should I not wake the Kommandant now, sir?"

"Wait until we get all we want from the others. This won't take long," Ingrassia said. We'll be back."

"This? Back from where?" the guard asked, as the last prisoner swept by him and climbed into the truck.

But his answer was lost to Luke's ears as the two vehicles' engines were already roaring

132

and heading towards the gate, which was still open.

They drove as fast as they dared away from the prison.

* * *

"The map, sir," Ingrassia said as they approached the crossroad. "This turn isn't on it."

"Hell," Captain Lomax breathed out. "Stop the car."

After he did, the men, rescuers and prisoners alike, formed a tight circle around the map Captain Lomax spread out over the trunk of the German car.

"Señor Castile," Luke addressed his ragged charge in the most formal Spanish he knew. "Would you kindly check our route to the beach at Donosti?" He carefully used the word both the Spanish and Basque people used for the port town of San Sebastian.

"Which beach?" Castile asked his own question, in English.

"Zurriola."

"Ah, the one which faces the open sea. A good choice. But your old map is useless." He smiled. "It is perhaps best that I take you there."

A grin broadened their leader's face.

"Were you in the diplomatic service before the war, Lieutenant Kayenta?" Lomax asked.

Luke glanced at Nantai, who rolled his eyes. "No, sir."

"To the sea, then, Señor Castile?" their leader asked.

"To the sea," the ragged man affirmed.

"They put a native guide on their liberation list. Smart move."

Arturo Castile and Luke exchanged a quick, amused glance.

"Ditch and camouflage the car. Everyone into the truck," Captain Lomax ordered.

* * *

From their next stop on a hilltop, the seaport town of San Sebastian and its three beaches stretched like dark crescent necklaces, like the ones Changing Woman demanded of the Sun as marriage gifts, Luke thought.

The water was a vast inky blackness punctuated by the lights of ships shining like stars in an almost empty universe. Only one star shone off Zurriola Beach.

Captain Lomax gave Luke his binoculars. "Were you trained in Morse Code, Lieutenant?"

"Yes, sir."

"Take a look. That's our ship, the Varian. And we're being hailed."

Luke felt a wave of euphoria as if he'd rounded the last bend in the trail before his mother's hogan. It startled him, feeling this in a strange land, brought on by winking lights from the vast sea.

"Signal them fast, Sarge, let 'em know what time we're coming," Ashton said. "I can smell a couple of Coney Island hot dogs now."

"Pile on the hash browns," Corbett added.

"Me, it's enough my girl's waiting on the dock in her red picture hat," Ingrassia contributed.

"And nothing else?" Havlish, this time.

"Hey, get your dirty mitts off my girl!"

"Enough," Captain Lomax reminded as their Sergeant signaled back with the lamp. "We're an ocean away, impersonating the enemy in hostile territory. Hide the truck, and then let's see if our contacts left us some seaworthy boats to row to our mother ship."

* * *

The checkpoint ahead was manned by six, all well-armed. Luke felt their spirits dive.

"I'm sorry," Castile whispered. "Donosti , that is, San Sebastian, is not so open as it once was."

"We are grateful for your assistance, Señor Castile."

Their guide nodded. Luke saw an unruly swatch of curl over his right ear. The man's daughter had the same curl, in the same place. Had the girl learned English from her father, he wondered.

Suddenly Castile's eyes brightened. "We are not without choice, however. I remember another way."

Their captain gave a quick nod.

Both the soldiers and the worn faces of the prisoners grew brightened with renewed hope.

Only after they were through the sharp-thorned hedges did they realize that their guide's rear entrance took them into one of San Sebastian''s graveyards.

Arturo Castile gave directions from there to the beach, shook Luke's hand and bowed before their captain, before he disappeared back into the night.

They rested, most leaning against the gravestones, which were worn and gray like great flat teeth, Luke thought. The winter cold blunted, but did not erase the scent of decay. Perhaps there was a fresh grave nearby.

Luke moved silently to Nantai. His clan brother's hand rested inside his opened coat. Luke knew his clan brother would not ask for help on his own.

"Corbett has bandaging."

"I need another kind of doctor."

"This is not like our for the dead places," Luke sought to reassure his friend. "People come, camp here, bring food. They like being close to their dead."

"Backward people," Nantai muttered in Dinè, but couldn't hide the fear from his voice. "I feel them," he whispered. "They're crying."

"This is a suffering country," Luke said. "It may be everyone cries, the living and the dead."

"I want to go home. Why did we think we would be good at this?"

"We need to rest, to heal, my brother. The world will look different then."

"Yes." Nantai's eyes scanned a line of stiff iron crosses. "It might be worse."

Sergeant Havlish approached them. "Captain wants us to meet behind that stone angel, sirs."

They followed Havlish to the gathering. The angel had beautiful downward spiraling wings, like Hawk's.

"All right, then," Captain Lomax began. "It's through town from now on." He marked the patch of dirt at his feet with a stick and continued. "We'll break into thirds behind each of our Spanish language speakers: Ingrassia, Riggs, and Kayenta; left flank, right flank, and down the middle. Avoid people. That would be only late revelers or early risers at this time of night. Our speakers are only for if we're directly addressed. Ingrassia, you're with me. Sergeant Havlish, with Riggs. The rest, count off to three."

Once he was satisfied with the mix of service men and escapees in each group, the captain continued. "Check your watches. Set them together. Our rendezvous with the Varian is set in forty minutes. We meet under the beach pier at exactly 0400 hours, understood? We've got help here. Rowboats will be waiting, I'm

137

told. If not, we steal what we need. We wait until then before embarkation. Are we clear?"

"Yes, sir," they whispered back, ghost voices in the graveyard.

Chapter 14

Luke saw the hitch in Nantai's walk become less pronounced, as the first two groups moved beyond the gates of the graveyard. How bad had his clanbrother's beating been, he wondered? Did Nantai have internal injuries?

He realized the first two groups were underway and his own was waiting for his direction. He turned his small band down the middle of the seaside town, catching the scent of salt on the wind, a warmer wind than in the mountains.

Buildings' second stories hung over the dark, quiet streets protectively. Luke kept his charges behind him in a casual line.

A woman stepped out of the shadows.

Her scent made Luke think of lush purple flowers. From her mouth came the lingering trail of hard cider along with her greeting.

"Saludos, querido mio."

She touched his face. "You have had a rough night already," she continued, in languid, Basque-accented Spanish.

"Verdad," he agreed.

"And now, you and your comrades are out after curfew."

"Curfew?" he repeated, hoping she would tell him more.

But she looked over her shoulder, into the courtyard beyond the rusting iron gate, and asked another question. "From where do you come?"

"The hills."

"Smugglers." She smiled. "Of people? Or material?"

"Both."

It seemed to please her, his ready admission. "Good," she said. "Lorca needs some competition."

Luke wanted to please her, as he always wanted to please women. Because they were beautiful, and powerful, as they were in all the creation stories of his people. This one spoke slowly, and did not berate his accent. Her jewelry, glistening bright red and blue beads danced between her breasts as she brushed her hair, a mass of black curls, back off her shoulder.

"Does your ship wait?"

"Yes."

"At which beach?"

"Zurriola."

She frowned like his sisters did when he voiced a stupid idea. "And you were about to parade past the new police station on your journey there?"

There was no police station on their map, or spoken of from Arturo Castile's memory. "Not now. We won't now," Luke said.

"No. You'll trust your Magdalena, will you not?"

Luke fought an urge, not only to trust her, but to rest his head between those beautiful breasts.

As if she'd heard his thought, she laughed softly. "I will guide you to your destination. You will not tell Lorca that I did so, however. And you will leave me a nice offering under the pier before you go, yes?"

"Si," he promised, remembering the remaining Spanish currency crammed into false bottom of the match box in his pocket. *"Gracias, Magdalena."*

"I like the sound of my name from your mouth, tall one. You and your silent mountain vagabonds may follow me."

Luke turned to his men and the released prisoners. Mort's eyes were wary. The rest looked like they had more confidence in Luke's judgment, or perhaps they were just more desperate. He could not think of how to tell them to trust this woman that he should not be trusting himself.

Luke nodded once, turned, and hoped they would shadow him.

They did.

Magdalena led them beyond the rusted gate and within a stone arched courtyard.

Luke sensed the prisoners' fear as they descended steps under the street level. Back underground, where they had been imprisoned for years. What was he doing? Allowing this woman to seduce him into a trap? If so, it would cause the ruination of not only himself, Ashton and Mort, but also the men Captain Lomax had put in their care.

He willed his breathing to lengthen, his thoughts to clear as he followed Magdalena's blue skirts. She seemed independent, like the women at home, herding their sheep, cooking over open fires, working their weavings for the good of their families.

The dampness of the cavernous space began to lift.

"Stay," their guide commanded.

They obeyed.

She went on alone.

"Lieutenant," Luke heard Mort's thin whisper in the darkness. "Where are we?"

"Close to the beach," he tried to assure them. "Smell the salt, the fish? And I hear the waves."

Magdalena's scent returned, then Magdalena herself. "The way is clear," she said.

Her lips grazed his cheek. She took his hand and led around one more curve in the stone wall.

Then she opened a low rounded wooden door.

The moon shone, casting shadows over Zurriola beach and the pier into the Bay of Biscay. An oilcloth tarp covered what Luke hoped were the promised boats, placed there for them to row out to the waiting ship Varian.

It looked like they were the first to arrive at Zurriola, thanks to this beautiful woman and her underground passage.

Magdalena nodded toward the short, balding prisoner from cell thirty-four. He had a small six-pointed star marked or tattooed on his cheek.

"That one. A Jew?"

Thirty-four. Morgenstern, Luke remembered, from Father Mikolas' etching into the sacred host. The man avoided her eyes but bowed graciously.

"My mother?" she told him softly, "what the Spanish call a Morrano."

The man bowed lower. "May God keep her in good health," he said.

Luke watched Magdalena's face harden like flint. "She's dead. Guernica. Our neighbors, they say she brought on the German bombs, because she was from a family that converted in name only. A family that still kept Passover sacred. Imagine that? She brought that hell down upon a city! My little mother, because she lighted candles."

Her eyes met Luke's. "Do not come back, my tall one. This country eats what is good and beautiful."

Her skirts disappeared into the passageway.

As the men walked toward the boats, Mort touched Luke's sleeve. "You were right about her, sir."

Luke heard the sudden slamming noise just before the beam of light hit the surf.

"Get down."

"What?"

"Hurry."

They followed his lead and ran for the shadows under the pier.

The beam passed and scanned the water beyond them.

"Where in hell did that come from??" Mort whispered.

Luke's head gestured as he reached into Ashton's pack. "A lighthouse, on that hill."

"Why did it go on just now, sir?"

"I don't know. Luke attached a sight to the Welrod. "What time is it?" he asked.

"Three-forty-eight, sir."

"Don't wait for me. Even if no one else comes, get the boat into the water at oh four hundred."

"But—"

"If I can't shoot the beam out, time its sweep. And get to the boat and on the water while you've got darkness helping you."

Ashton's shoulders fell. "Yes, sir. Good luck, sir."

"And to all of you," he told the men in his charge, realizing it was a Catholic Mass response from his altar boy days. "*Dominus vobiscum*," said the priest. "*Et cum spiritu tuo*," he had answered. The Lord be with you. And with your spirit.

As he watched the arc of light, he rifled for the match box deep in his coat. He took the money from the false bottom and left his offering for their guide Magdalena beside a piling. Magdalena, Luke thought. Wasn't that the name of one of Jesus' friends? The prostitute turned saint?

He worked his way to the rock wall then walked along it until he found the steep stairs that led to the base of the lighthouse.

He saw the beam combing the shore.

At the base, two police motorcycles were parked. "Damn!" Luke whispered, startling himself. The Dinè people had no curses, but he had heard a few while in training. He and Nantai had been raised to be tolerant of other people's behavior, so up until now he accepted the practice with a shrug. He'd never used any of the words himself. But here, now, it felt good on his tongue. He began to understand why the *belegaana* used curses. He wished he remembered more.

Now, think. If he could get some distance, and use the Welrod to silence his shot, it might seem as if the lamp blew out naturally. He would then need time to get back to his men on the beach.

He surveyed the hill. Gnarled wind-blown trees offered no cover.

Luke judged only one spot with a chance at a decent angle — a ruin of an arched wall, there in the dark, standing like a guardian rock in a canyon at home.

If he could find enough footholds, perhaps it would do. He checked his watch. Three-fifty-five.

Would there be enough time to get back?

Chapter 15

Like the canyons of home, there was no mortar between the stones of the wall. Its footholds were regular, cut by men. Luke climbed, sighted his target.

He didn't know how strong the glass protecting the lighthouse lamp's filament was. Or if his shot would have any effect. But the light swept the beach, where his comrades were gathering, not the sea. It was looking for them. So he had to try.

Luke checked the silencer, aimed, and fired.

The kickback came after only a strangled burst of sound. Louder was the breaking glass.

Then, black darkness. Luke smothered a cry of triumph.

A burst of machine gun fire riddled the rock face above his head. Someone had figured his location. A good marksman, armed with a weapon that could cast death like the beam cast light.

Luke froze.

What would the gunman do next? *Think.* He would know he'd missed, and strafe lower.

Luke remembered his evasive maneuver training. He jumped, hitting the sand, rolling forward in what he hoped was not a straight line.

The smell of salt grew stronger. He must keep moving, it was his only chance.

The beach was beautiful, waiting, welcoming.

Too quiet. Tarps waved in the cold winter breeze. He wanted a place in a boat. He wanted to go home. But there was nothing under the tarps.

Luke took cover under the pier, yanked out the chain looped outside his vest pocket and opened his grandfather's watch.

0200-10.

He was too late. Too late, for he was traveling in Indian time, not by the watch, taking enough of it to get his task done, without considering the sweep of the seconds, the minute hand. Not closely. Not closely enough.

The Dinè had no word for time.

Why did they think they would be good at this?

There. He saw the fishing boats with the deep hulled bottoms out on the water. One, then another. Leaving without him, as he'd told them to. Crammed with men. More than they'd planned to rescue, perhaps, because of a kind-hearted priest, and a little girl who missed her father.

Safe, they were almost safe.. He'd done his job.

Luke smiled, searching out the horizon. There, the ship Varian, like a welcoming mother.

Finally he spotted one more small boat, still on shore, but with its nose already in the surf, waiting. A dark head popped up behind it.

Nantai.

"Come on, Monster Slayer," he called softly. "I'm not going home without you."

Luke ran forward, grabbing for the back of the boat. A burst of gunfire splintered the wood.

"Push," Nantai said, firing off two covering shots. Luke felt the water seep above his boot tops.

More gunfire. Then a voice demanded their surrender.

But Luke only listened to his clan brother.

"Get in," Nantai said in his familiar, unhurried drawl. Nantai was a slow talker, even among the slow talker Navajo people.

Luke used one leg to spring, yanking the other one over the side. He saw the stars, glorious, like those of home.

"Now help me," Nantai said.

Where?

Desert dwellers, neither of them could swim. Their trainers in California had just managed to teach them to float, and not give in to their own fear. Luke grasped his clan brother's arm and heaved the rest of him into the boat.

"Moon's out, helping, we need to move fast," Nantai said, scrambling for an oar.

Luke found the other. His friend had already claimed the more vulnerable side.

Bullets made pings and gashes in the water. One of the Americans' two boats was coming back, drawing some of the fire.

Nantai laughed, as if they were on their way to a Green Corn Dance.

Then a thud, and something landed between Luke's feet. A rock, with a tail, that was on fire. An explosive.

Luke grabbed it, tossed it in the air, kicked it, as he did many times during ball games on community days at home. This ball he kicked hard as he could.

He caught a quick glimpse of the Varian. Then the explosion took away everything— his sight, his hearing, his hold on the earth beneath a new water world.

Chapter 16

The rolling water turned Luke over, then popped him above the waves. He grabbed at air and something that might have been Nantai's sleeve, but the water foamed over and he lost his grip.

He yielded to the force that was so much greater than he, hearing his California instructor's voice: *"Don't panic, you crazy Indians!"* He was rewarded with the reassuring feel of earth beneath his feet. He stood. Yes, he still had legs. And beside him, sputtering, on his knees, was Nantai. He pulled his clan brother to the shoreline.

The waves had deposited them farther down from the wreckage of their boat, away from their pursuers. Busy examining the splintered wood, the men argued.

"Just as well."

"No! This is not what the Germans wanted! Alive! The Germans wanted them alive! They will flay us, now that those two are food for the fish."

Except they were not food for the fish, Luke thought. They were alive.

They could find the woman in the beautiful skirts, Magdalena. She would hide them; Luke knew she would.

He looked up at the sky, at the clouds covering the moon, keeping them invisible. Nantai moaned. Luke leaned over him.

"My brother, listen. If we get to that break wall, climb over it, we will have a chance. Get up."

"I lost my boot."

The lost item stood stiff, at attention, in the surf. Luke almost laughed. "We are Dinè! We don't need boots!"

Nantai moaned again.

Luke's gaze shifted to the thing in the surf. It was stiff. And too tall.

Nothing was below Nantai's right knee, except a river of blood.

Heart line blood.

"Never mind, my brother. Stay still," Luke breathed out, yanking off his belt, tying it tight above the blood river, to cut off the flow.

Crouched under his friend's chest, Luke took Nantai across his shoulders.

He must get to the break wall.

He would think about what to do next once he got there. One foot in front of the other, until then.

Closer. He could see the rocks, neatly stacked without bonding mortar, illuminated. By what? The moon, free again of the clouds, betraying them.

Spanish voices called for them to stop.

"Keep going," Nantai said quietly.

Luke was not one, but two, with the other Monster Slayer, his twin. He was pulled by the moon's light, by the courage of his brother, to reach those rocks.

The voices called again.

Luke braced for the gunshots. They did not come. Nothing came except footfalls in the sand, except the pumping of his heart in his ears.

The grey rocks of the break wall came so close he could see salt stains from the tide.

They would be there soon. Then what? He must think. He must think of what to do then.

He felt a sharp blast behind his knees, pitching him forward.

He wanted to tell Nantai to hold on, because they were going down. But he landed hard, buried beneath the sand, beneath Nantai.

He crawled. Nantai's weight lifted.

Bereft, he focused on disgusted voices, saying things that made no sense,. Luke realized that he no longer understood English or Spanish or Dinè or any language. Only music, his first language. He heard only that music. The music of the long-ago beating of his mother's heart in the blackness.

And he saw only his own fingers, still crawling through the sand.

Chapter 17

He knew the figure. Balding, ragged Kokopeli, the trickster spirit.

"Open your mouth, son. There, good. Now swallow. Go on. Don't die of thirst. That would be a hell of a thing, after all you've been through, to die of thirst, eh? Hey, listen, and have some pity. If you go, I go, see? On account of I told them I could get you up and running."

The trickster shook his head.

"Kokopeli." Luke heard his own voice, but yes, dry, and raspy. "Sing."

"What?"

"A spell song."

"A prayer, you mean?"

What kind of Kokopeli was he, to have to be told his own business, Luke thought impatiently.

Kokopeli's singing was not in Dinè, but it won. It helped him navigate over the stench, the dampness.

"Thank you," Luke breathed out, when the song ended. His throat worked again. It helped him swallow the liquid the trickster spirit put to his lips.

Humor returned to the deep-set eyes of Kokopeli, who was not Kokopeli, but a small man, dressed in grey rags, scarred around his ear, through the bridge of his nose, and across one of those eyes full of mischief. It was as if some monster had been playing with the locations of his features and they were slowly finding their way home again. Two front teeth were black and another chipped. But when he smiled, his whole face lifted into beauty.

"Listen, my *shepseleh*. I make myself useful with what I got for you — a little mint leaf, a little honey, a little salt concoction. To help you back into the world of the living! Not that you'd say of the quality, 'This? This is living?' Why? Because you proved what I been saying for years. And what is that? That we can crack this rotten joint, that's what! I gotta meet this guy, says I. So, I puff up my skills a little, so what?"

"Yes. So what?" Luke tried to slow down the crazy beautiful music of Kokopeli man's speech.

"So, you're feeling better now, right?"

"*Lanh*. Right."

"Hey, *tateleh*, the guards say you gave away your chance of escape."

"I did not give it away. I gave it to Nantai. There's a difference."

"Of course there is. A *mitzvah*, you did, my friend. I'm proud to make your acquaintance."

Those kind eyes. Keeping his terror at bay.

154

"And who am I, you ask? Why Sergeant Isaiah Morgenstern of the Lincoln Brigade, but once upon a time of apartment 4G, above the clock shop at 96 Orchard Street, Lower East Side of the island of Manhattan. And this friend of the honored Nantai is— ?"

"Lieutenant Luke Kayenta, of postal box twenty, Riordan Station, Arizona," he followed the man's protocol.

"Oh, ho! Arizona, is it? You are a wild west cowboy soldier, then, far away from your home on the range?"

Luke scowled. "Sheep. The people of Dinetah...Navajo country--we herd sheep, not cows!"

"*Oy, Zay moykhi!* Please forgive me, dear child of the forest free!"

Luke laughed out loud at his own indignation. "Desert. My home is in the American desert, sir."

Sergeant Morgenstern smiled wide. "Yes, I see that I have a lot to learn from you, my tall red man *bubaleh.* But now, by the grace of God and the hospitality of our stinking fascist hosts, we are both of cell thirty-four."

"Thirty-four?" Luke remembered the silly rhyme attached to the number, and the name. "Morgenstern was one of those Americans we rescued. Why—?"

"Getting a boil removed. From my *tuches*... posterior. At the infirmary. So my cellmate took my place, I gather. Got put in my cell as punishment, and branded with a star of David to

155

boot, by some bored guard, though he's as Catholic as the pope himself! Can't blame him for not letting on. But how's that for luck? I missed all the excitement. The ship, you say? How many made it to the ship?"

"All of the prisoners and the rescue team except us — Nantai and me."

"Ah, *mechaya koontz*! That is: a delicious accomplishment!"

It was, Luke realized. He should give thanks for it. But first he must find his clan brother.

"Sergeant Morgenstern, you were in the infirmary. Did you see my companion? He was hurt. Did they bring Nantai there?"

"No. But they hauled me in here for questioning pretty soon after you came on board with us, Bunkie. Maybe they put your friend there."

Sergeant Morgenstern rose from his low, three legged stool. "How about more of my nice tea? Cool you are now, *boychik*, but *oy,* were you ever s*chvitzing*!"

"Schv—?"

"Sweating," he translated. "What? No Yiddish spoken where you come from?" He brought a single candle close to Luke without missing a conversational beat. "Well, I'll teach you a whole mishmash of Yiddish. Words that capture volumes! Expressions to make your point with gleaming brilliance." His voice softened. "Endearments to melt the hardest woman's heart."

"And curses?"

Isaiah Morgenstern's damaged eyebrow almost disappeared into the wrinkles of surprise on his forehead. "It's curses you want, my *kemfer*?"

"Yes. My language has no curses. I might need some here."

The man's chuckle was light, like everything else about him. "Listen, by our own bust-out time, you'll be a regular *meyvin* of curses!"

Chapter 18

"So. You're a *nosher*, my friend."

"*Nosher*?"

"Nibbler. An eater of small meals. The meal is a *nosh*, so is the verb, the act of eating it. And the eater a *nosher*, get it?"

Luke nodded as he finished off the empanada. "At home, we *nosh*, too. The women keep the stew pot going all day. We eat when we're hungry. Until we feel full. Except at feast times."

Sergeant Morgenstern smiled. "And what happens then?"

"We do too much of everything. We dance, play games and gamble, and eat and eat and eat."

"Ah, until you *plats*!"

"*Plats*?"

"Burst! From *plotz*, which means to burst. You think yours are the only people who know how to have a good time?"

"No. I did not mean to say that. I'm sorry."

Isaiah Morgenstern swatted the air of their cell. "*Nishtkefelecht!* It's you should be complaining of my company, my quiet friend. I'm a New York Jew used to yelling over traffic.

I'm not angry or offended, just loud. You got some luck in roommates, bunkie."

"Yes," Luke agreed. "Good luck. I am too serious. The women tell me that all the time."

"You pay close attention to your women, do you?"

Luke smiled. "Well. They are good with knives."

Isaiah Morgenstern laughed out of his mouth and nose together. Luke liked that laugh, it signaled that he was both surprised and amused.

"I should stop thinking of your females as *shiksas*," he said. "My considered opinion: the Lost Tribes? From one boat landed in Arizona, maybe?"

"We have no shoreline. And it is said we came from underground," Luke countered.

"Mole people, yours? You don't look like any subway straphanger I ever saw, *yingel.*"

Yingel. Pupik. Boyhik. bubaleh. Tateleh. Shepseleh. Isaiah had so many names for him! All endearments, given to treasured children, he assured Luke. But if he'd been called so many names as a child, he doubted he'd ever learn his real one.

Isaiah Morgenstern was as crafty as the hump-backed flute player. How long had he been listening to his Kokopeli, who was full of questions, who answered questions with questions in verbal dances like those of his own people? Luke looked at the marks he'd

159

scratched on the cell wall beside his bed. Four days.

"Just digesting, *shepseleh*?"

"Digesting?"

Morgenstern shook his head. "No, no. Listen. Just repeating the same question is not so good as: 'And which fellow skeleton wants to know?' or 'I can help the workings of my own digestive tract, you're thinking?' Get it?"

"What? You think I am stupid?"

"Good! That's good! It will help. Believe me, when these *mamzers* try to get anything out of you, see? Keep playing ignorant, full of the questions, like we do now, for fun. Now, about that quiet percolating going on behind your bedroom eyes — are you hatching an escape plan?"

Luke shrugged. "Who wouldn't be?"

"Ha! Good, *tateleh*! And I'll help you to get the lay of this labyrinth that is Hell Hole inside the revered Porta Coeli. Then, when your friends come back for you, you'll lead the rest of us republicans and Basque nationals out of here."

"I doubt they will be sending anyone."

"Why not?"

"Nantai and I — we are not regular army," Luke said slowly, considering his words, careful not to admit to Isaiah Morgenstern that he and his clan brother were in a branch of the service that was itself a secret, that was about spying. They killed spies, right away. He and Nantai's only hope was to keep up their cover as shepherds testing a new enterprise in their mountains. Would the small man tell their captors Luke had given away his rank, and that he was a Navajo?

Footsteps. More than the usual patrol. And alarm in his cellmate's eyes.

"Lie down, bunkie. Eyes closed. Let me do the talking."

Luke obeyed, as he had several times before. But there was something different about the precise sound of these boots.

The room crowded with colliding scents of leather, wool, and anger. Sergeant Morgenstern began his rapid-fire Spanish, explaining Luke was sleeping, that they both needed better food, some time outside.

Luke felt a shake at his shoulders.

He looked into the hard black eyes of an officer. "You will come with us."

Isaiah Morgenstern stepped forward. "I'm telling you, this is a sick man! Let it be on your heads if —"

The officer landed a punch that sent Kokopelli reeling against the wall.

Before he could advance further, Luke bolted up and stood between them, his arms braced.

Two guards quickly pinned him against the wall.

The officer smiled. "So, you are not so bad off. The Jew has proven himself useful."

* * *

Luke counted the steps up the stairway until he and the guards were above ground.

Once the thick wooden door to the courtyard was unbolted, the guards moved him too fast, dragging while he blinked in the unfamiliar, intense sunlight. He tried to memorize the yard's dimensions, the number and positions of guards on the wall.

The monastic infirmary was in the building to the west, Isaiah had said. Regain your stride, keep up, Luke told himself. Perhaps Nantai was watching, from a window. Don't give him more to worry about.

They passed twisted stone columns shaped like snaking vines around the trunk of a tree. Isaiah told him they had been holding up the tiled roof for centuries. The oldest part of the monastery-turned-prison, was in the style named for the ancient people, the Romans, with its arches and pillars.

* * *

An automobile stood before the building they were heading toward, a long, black automobile, its uniformed chauffeur standing beside it.

Luke remembered Isaiah's map of the complex, which he had drawn in the dirt floor of their cell. They were entering what had once been a small chapel, but was now the office of the commander. Embedded deep in the massive stone, two round stained glass windows let some sunlight into the room. Light shone on a man in a beautifully tailored dark suit and polished nails, holding soft leather gloves, and a fedora hat; a man so different, so out of place in this world.

"You are better, Señor Kayenta?" he asked in proper, Castilian Spanish.

"Yes, thank you."

"I arrived from Madrid as soon as I could. Please," he indicated the lone straight backed wooden chair, "sit."

When Luke hesitated, a guard shoved him down. The polished Spaniard frowned slightly, waved him back and concentrated again on Luke. "I am a diplomatic envoy. Your employer is very concerned about you. Your comrade, Señor Riggs—"

"Where is he?"

A rifle butt hit the stone floor. "No questions! Only answers!"

A man in a double breasted wool uniform coat entered the room, filling it with his presence. His head of closely cropped greying hair was bare and his military hat tucked under his arm.

"I was reviewing the guards advanced training outside our walls, Consul," he said bowing stiffly. "Or else I would have been here to welcome you." He cast a furious look toward Luke "The prisoner is not bound or chained!" he shouted at the guards.

"Yes. At my request, sir," the diplomat said with a steely softness.

A twitch in the uniformed man's cheek made the deep creases beside it even deeper. This is a person who has been displeased most of his life, Luke thought. "You should not have begun without me, Consul."

The smaller man nodded. "Thank you for your concern, *El Director.* But I assure you, I believe myself in no danger from this simple shepherd."

The prison's director was not able to hide his anger over the consul commanding action in his absence. But the polished gentleman gave no indication that he was aware of the director's fury. His voice stayed steady and cordial. "I am learning that Señor Kayenta is only concerned about his wounded friend. Perhaps we could grant the two a reunion?"

"Impossible! They are both classed as *incommunicado* and dangerous, sir."

This was the prison director, who had slept through the entire escape, Luke realized. He had no first-hand knowledge of the operation of Captain Lomax and his men, and the reports from the night's prison guards might have been muddled. Nantai drove the truck. But it had all happened so fast, perhaps Nantai's face was lost in the crowd. Was there a way out of this for them?

The tailored man lifted three fingers, as a priest does in blessing.

The director retreated from the room, a move that had the guards staring at each other in wonder.

The consul turned his attention back to Luke. "I'm afraid I do not meet with everyone's approval here, just as you do not, yes? They are used to the most hardened of criminals, traitors, anarchists, you see. Kindly allow me to resume the lead in our discussion. But be assured. We in Madrid have cordial relations with Señor Spenser and his companies. Your friend Señor Riggs is being looked after."

Luke nodded, grateful.

The diplomat began to walk a slow circle around Luke's chair. The colored glass threw rainbows over his beautiful white suit of clothes.

"Now, your employer the esteemed Señor Spencer speaks of his high regard, and his wish to have you both back in the bosom of his care since your unfortunate experience here. He is sure all evidence will prove circumstantial, that you and Señor Riggs were... hostages on the night of the uprising."

He stood still before Luke, one hand over the one holding his fine hat and gloves. Their clench deepened. "First, I must report on your condition. Have you been harmed in any way within these walls?"

"No, sir."

"And has anyone taken clothes or possessions from you?"

"No."

"Good. And they will not. You and the shepherd Señor Riggs are our guests. Now, let us work together so that this unpleasantness between Spain and the United States of America might cease. I will do my part. But you must do yours. And I'm afraid the authorities are insisting you have some time alone to consider your answers to questions they are formulating."

"Might I see the other shepherd? He was hurt. I don't remember well, but he was bleeding, you see."

Luke watched those polished, tapping fingers. They stopped.

"Ah, no. I fear not."

Then the diplomat turned, and left.

The room was empty of everything but the faint scent of incense. And the echoing of centuries of holy chanting,. And screams.

Chapter 19

Luke knew cell thirty-two, deep under the complex of courtyard, cloister, chapels. refractory and infirmary. It was the smallest square on Captain Lomax's map. There was no window. Fresh straw, but streaks on the wall. Letters, words, disintegrating to fragments of babble. When the door closed, not even that.

Blackness, like in a cave.

He could not stand to his full height.

Nantai could have. Nantai would do better in here, as he would have in the confining spaces of the missionary school when they were children.

This was a school, too. A school, and he was sent to the corner for not doing his number recitations fast enough, that's all. A corner. Not all four walls, closing in to crush him, to steal his soul.

They would laugh about this later, he and Nantai. They would tell their friend who had endured years in this place, Isaiah Morgenstern, that it was not worse than that school, no worse than the punishments of that straight-backed teacher who called her students heathens. No worse than the matron with her boar's hair brush, scrubbing their teeth and gums and tongue with Fels Naptha soap for the crime of talking to each other in Navajo, after dark, under their threadbare blankets. Scrubbing as she yelled, "English only, English only!" so loudly that the youngest ones woke, afraid and crying for their mothers, their grandmothers, their sheep. Scrubbing so hard, but he did not cry, and laughed when she left and he told stories to the little ones until they went back to sleep. And they did not forget their language even though they could not taste food for days after their scrubbings.

And now he and Nantai and the other warriors they taught to work the radios, to use their Dinè words in code, they might help win a war because their language was not scrubbed from their hearts.

No, he could not tell Isaiah that, not any of that. Top secret.

When he dozed, Luke heard his clan brother singing a healing song. *That's right my brother, sing towards your return, to wellness, to balance and beauty, to Dinetah. I will see you soon. And we will return. We will go home.*

But was it his clan brother's voice, or his own longing?

Crawling beings crept onto the roots of his hair. They didn't stay long with him there, in the dark. Not enough there to feed on, maybe. Or he was not to their taste. Would mice or rats come here too? Or were there no openings wide enough for them? He stretched whatever allowed it- his shoulder, his arms, the muscles of his face.

Should he take his boots off, let his feet, at least, be free? Nantai took one of his boots off, didn't he? There on the beach? Luke couldn't quite remember.

The boots were made in Sweden, with eight metal eyelets and a leather toe cap. All weather boots, light, waterproof, with corrugated soles. And full of secret places, thanks to the English spymasters. No, better not to take them off, they were more than boots. One held a cyanide capsule. He would crush it between his teeth if he had to. But also in hiding, in another compartment, was the airman's letter to his wife, reminding Luke he had promises to keep.

* * *

Two guards came. They brought Luke on a winding journey to a domed chamber. This room was not on any of the Americans' maps. It was large, but with no windows, no view of the sky or light coming through stained glass.

Fear crept beneath his skin. He must concentrate. On his interrogator, sitting in a carved high back chair against a wall, lit only by an oil lamp in a sconce. It was the angry Spanish director of Porta Coeli prison, the one who had not disguised his contempt for the diplomat in the beautiful suit. That one was not here. No matter. That one could not be trusted, despite his patrician airs and well-modulated voice.

One of the guards released him there, in the center of the room. Luke lost his balance, not used to standing, but regained it quickly. Their superior posted them on either side of the door. One turned the wick of the oil lamp higher. It helped reflect the light on the gold braiding at the director's shoulders.

Luke looked up. A heavy chain hung from the room's domed ceiling. It had once been frescoed, that ceiling. He caught sight of the remains of an angel's wing.

He remembered his training. Passive. Keep all face features calm. They feed on your expression. He did not think it would be so difficult. Hadn't it been what his people had been doing for generations of enduring the encroachments on their land and souls? By the Spanish, the French, the Mexicans, the Americans?

The director's voice was calm, but had a steely tension beneath it. "Why do you protect them? They blew up your boat. Caused your partner such suffering."

They were not left behind. The boat had been coming back for them. Until the explosion. All Luke remembered was the ball with a tail landing at his feet in the boat. Had it come from the shore? But where would light keepers or local police get explosives, like the one he himself had used, hidden within the flashlight?

Not Magdalena. He would have caught the scent of gunpowder on her. Had someone else betrayed them? Someone they thought a friend?

"Now," his interrogator said, "tell me about the interesting weapons that washed up on the beach."

"Weapons? We are shepherds, sir. We have only what we need to protect the sheep."

The officer sighed. A small sound that terrified Luke. "Ah, Spenser's shepherd. Your own protector has gone. He has left you to me. You must not waste my time. It will only cause you pain. There are missing German officers on holiday that no one seems to be able to find. Not even their bodies, imagine. There was the first escape from this prison in one hundred and fifty-three years. I need names. Collaborators."

A nod and the guard's boot landed a blow to his jaw. It opened the wound on his lip, the one Isaiah Morgenstern's concoctions had fought so hard to heal. Luke fell to his knees as his mouth filled with blood. He breathed fiercely out of his nostrils.

Go away from it, from the scent of iron, of centuries of suffering in this airless room. Against the opposite wall, Luke saw a tongueless man, laughing, at the same thing Luke found amusing. They demanded a confession then made it impossible to speak.

He was there, and was not there, the man. Like fog. Was it someone's *chindi*, an evil spirit trapped here, not able to disperse? Or perhaps the evil had snuck out that small door, and the tongueless man had left his *yeii,* whose beautiful white wing was still painted on the ceiling?

The second soldier yanked him up from the stone floor by his hair. Their commander came close enough for Luke to see the fine crease in his uniform's trousers.

Together, the two guards attached his writs to the chain hanging from the ceiling.

Suddenly, they backed away, without an order from their commander. Luke swayed, dizzy with pain. What were they seeing? Perhaps the tongueless man?

The director's voice hardened, and lost its unnatural calm. "I will tell your advocate from Madrid the disappointing news, Señor Kayenta. He will not be pleased."

To the soldiers he said, "Continue."

* * *

Adler cupped his hand to one ear and spoke over the long-distance phone lines.

"Did you ask about the radio transmissions? The language they spoke?"

A silence.

"No, not Mexicans,. They are Indians. Red American Indians! Radio transmissions between the two of them, in the mountains!" Adler yelled into the receiver.

More silence.

He could hear the Spaniard's deep intake of breath before his voice crackled across the wires. "Herr Adler, we are in the middle of

172

diplomatic pandemonium concerning these men. And we are attempting to discover what led to a well-armed escape of prisoners in a facility that has not yielded a single fugitive since Scottish and Danish merchant heretics were being questioned by the last inquisition! "

"I don't care to hear about your own people's stupidity! You must find out the language those two spoke to each other!"

"Be assured, sir. If the radio chatter is so important to our friends of the Reich, we will intensify our efforts. Our guest will soon be begging us to accept testimony in any language you require."

"What are you saying? What have you done?"

"Perhaps you would be so good as to return General Brinkerhoff to the line, please?"

Adler flung the phone's receiver down on the mahogany desktop. So. Franco's little *schwuchtel* diplomat thought he could pull rank?

Enough. He would go to Himmler himself now.

* * *

Luke counted the steps more precisely this time. And he knew the turns in the walls better. He could help the Americans or English to map it now.

The chair was gone. So was the tongueless man. Had those ceiling chains once held a source of light? Had light had ever been part of this room? He caught a buried scent— incense. There must have been light of course, long ago, when this part of the building honored the Christian god, who the missionaries told him was the same as Creator, who loved him, and wanted him to do good work.

Luke couldn't find that long ago sacred time, not through all the fear, the deep dread of the others, so many others before him, waiting, as he was now, for what they were about to do. He closed his eyes and lived on memories shaped there in the dark. His grandmother's hands at her weaving, his mother's sad eyes following the sudden east wind on the day he left home.

Then dreams began. Yes, he told himself, ignore the rest, what they were doing — taking off his boots, all his clothes except for the loose shepherd's undergarment. Breaking the diplomat's promise, that nothing would be taken from him. He needed his boots. The capsule was there. And the airman's letter. The capsule was not important, if they meant to kill him here. But the letter, that should not be found if it could not get to the one it was meant for. Never mind. There was nothing he could do. Except live here, inside the dreams.

In one his niece Iris watched the daughter of Arturo Castile wear her first smile gift proudly to church.

In another, the airman's wife stood, facing the ocean, swaddled in bright colors with a large purple flower behind her ear. Was it the beach at

San Sebastian? Go away from there, soaked in Nantai's blood. No, another beach, of fine golden sand. She waited there. Not for him, it couldn't be for him.

He didn't know the place, scented with a perfumed mist. It must be a dream of hers that he had invaded. That was rude. He should leave.

But then she turned, said his name, not her husband's. It banished his fear of her disappointment. He approached those beautiful arms, glowing like the moon. He traced her side with his hand, cupped the curve of her hip covered with soft red cotton, printed with swirling pictures of more flowers. He eased her down on the sand, drinking the scents of her salt-tinged body.

She stroked his hair, traced his red burn scars with her tongue, healing them. Then she welcomed him between her thighs as if they'd been lovers forever.

An odd, discordant thought invaded the waves of pure physical pleasure. *Scars?*

And then he caught the scent of burning flesh.

"Names. You understand? We need all the names. And how the prison break operation was accomplished. That first, before you speak that language you spoke over your radios, and tell us why this is so important to the Germans."

He strangled a cry. He was bound to those hooks in the ceiling. Not a lamp. Not incense, or anything holy. Him. He saw the glowing red tip, there in the dark.

"*Momzer. Schlump. Shitik drek,*" he called them. Untrustworthy bastard. Pathetic. Shithead.

"No. I am not interested in your secret language, save that for the Germans! I want names!"

When would it stop? When would the iron rods finish? When they'd tattooed around his middle, the way mindless people carved into tree bark, killing it?

Or would they press the glowing iron deeper? Would it go through his muscle, ligaments, beyond? Would they sear his bones?

He felt himself gagging. *Replace the smell, find another.* Sage, burning; weaving its way around the fingers of a holy man. He watched sand appearing between fingers, healing. Colored sand, not the deep colors of the stained glass of their churches, but of the painted desert of home.

Nantai, his mind cried out, *I'm not good at this.*

"You are doing well, my brother."

He opened his eyes. Not soon enough. Where was Nantai?

His throat throbbed. From the curses Isaiah Morgenstern had taught him? Or had he called out for his clan brother?

They were smiling, his tormentors.

A meshugener zol men oyshraybn, un im araynshraybn, Luke thought out one of Isaiah's Yiddish curses in their general direction. How

176

did it go? They should free a madman, and lock them up instead.

"Your friend has already confessed. How else do we know about your secret language? Why are you so stubborn? Don't you want to see him? He needs you. He is very sick."

Nantai, at his ear. "Lies. Hold on. Almost done."

The scent of his flesh burning finally made what little was in his stomach come up, spill over. His manacled hands couldn't wipe it away.

Think of another curse, quickly. One came into his mind — *A rud zol dir ariber iber dee gehirn* – may a wheel run over your skull. The torturers laughed, as if he'd said it out loud. Then they put their irons to the vomit. Smoke. Fire. Their faces began to break apart and swim in a blackening sea. The mouth of one slid to the other's shoulder.

The door opened.

The tongueless man appeared, hovering unsteadily on his one angel's wing. He raised very broken fingers to Luke's eyes, and closed the lids.

"*Meirda!*" Luke heard the commander curse quietly. "Bring him down. Let the Jew clean up the mess."

* * *

The next thing Luke was conscious of was the sound of scraping. His cellmate, dragging his thumbnail along the wall.

He opened his eyes. The sound stopped.

"What is it with you desert people? Are you some kind of crazy lizard?"

"Gila monster."

"What?"

"Water and fat storage. In his tail. The gila monsters. Those are the ones who live in my homeland."

A laugh, from his Kokopelli. Just the sound he had been waiting for.

"You have to drink, Lieutenant."

Candlelight. Kind eyes, after all the mocking ones. Yes. He drank from those scarred hands.

"Did you hear him singing, I don't know when, maybe in the night?" Luke asked his friend.

"Who, *shepseleh*?"

"The one they brought in with me. Nantai."

"No, my friend. I'm sorry, no."

"They allow you to put me back together. Why did they not ask you to help him too? You are a good healer. He's very sick. In the infirmary, they said. You were in the infirmary, Sergeant Morgenstern. Are you sure you did not see him there?"

"No, Luke."

"I have to get him out."

"You have to survive first. Ach! You put up with more than a little *utzing*, today, maybe?

178

That's why they put you back in the bosom of my care? Got you wrapped, put back together, as you say. How does the middle feel?"

"Like it's on fire."

"This does not surprise me. Swallow, please, my *yingel*."

Sergeant Morgenstern's tea, sluicing over his lips, stinging through his mouth, and down his throat. "Nantai's worse. His leg, you see? He could not get up, run with me. That's how I remember it. Blood. I had to carry him. He was hurt. Not by our men, our own men. Lies. Those were lies. But I have to get him out soon, before they start doing to him what they're doing to me."

Too much. Was he talking too much? He grabbed the man's shirtfront. "It is all right, to tell you this?"

"What kind of *misigas* is that? Of course it's all right. We'll get out together, my *kemfer*. I'm sharpening my weapon." He smiled, holding up his thumb and its yellowed nail, which came to a very sharp looking point. "There. A secret I'll trust with you, this weapon. We'll use it to get ourselves free. Or die together, trying. How would that be, my friend?"

Luke leaned back. "A delicious accomplishment. A *mechaya koontz*."

Then, that everyday miracle Luke had learned to cherish: Isaiah Morgenstern's laughter. "Welcome home, my young friend. I missed the way you mangle my language."

179

"I need more curses."

"*Gey shlofn,*" Isaiah said softly. "You know I been carving a list of them here for years. On the wall and now in your mouth to hurl at those ugly *mamzers*. Latest editions, for your reading pleasure."

Luke limped closer to the wall. He scanned the writings, which began with simple insults like "go peddle your fish elsewhere" and "drop dead" and "so you think you're a *k'nacker,* a big shot," to the colorful curses like *shteyner af zayne beyner*, "stones on his bones" and *Trinkn zoln im piavkes* — "leeches should drink him dry," to the deeply taboo ones, even for a people as oppressed by so many for so long as the Jews. Luke began to memorize the fresh ones.

Then he realized his feet were bare. Panic ignited his veins. His breath caught in his throat.

"Where are my boots?"

"Take it easy, my young friend. They are here, returned, along with your slightly diminished self."

"I need them. I need to put them on, keep them on, until we're gone from this place. Or dead."

"You want to die with your boots on. Are you sure you're not a cowboy, *shepseleh*?"

Chapter 20

Kitty watched the skaters gliding around Central Park Lake, with Belvedere Castle, now a weather station, rising up and giving the snowy Sunday a fairyland quality. She remembered being as care-free as Zala, her sister's ten year-old, who was forming a whip with her cousins Dominic and Matty, her brother Matthew's boys. Thinking of her brothers and Papa teaching her to ice skate was easier than thinking of Philippe, so natural on the ice after growing up among the frozen lakes and ponds of Quebec. He'd taught her some of the moves he'd learned from the Canadian champions Montgomery Wilson and Constance Wilson Samuel, their axel and lutz. She'd worked hard on them, to please him, to look beautiful in his eyes. He knew she would be an accomplished figure skater, he'd told her, because she was such a good dancer, and because she took such athletic relish when they made love. And once the lesson was over he would a hum a waltz at her ear while they glided in figure eights around the ice. All their fellow skaters would clear a path for them, just like the dancers did in the Fred Astaire and Ginger Rodgers musicals.

Well, so much for keeping those memories at bay.

Kitty pulled her attention back to her nephews and niece. She'd showed Philippe's figures to Zala, who was now trying to teach her cousins. Patiently, as the boys preferred the speed of their whip.

"Get your toes more pigeoned and draw your arms close next time Matty, you've almost got a good lutz! Hasn't he, Aunt Kitty?" she called.

"Yes," Kitty called back to them. "Almost."

"She's a natural teacher, my Zala is, don't you think?" Anya proclaimed more than asked, so Kitty thought a smile would suffice in reply.

Her mother put her arm around her youngest daughter's shoulder. "In a few years, you'll be out on the ice with your little one, who will master all those fancy moves," she said quietly at her ear.

Kitty nodded. But she couldn't see it. She'd always had a good imagination, but she couldn't see it. She was not worried about being a mother, or even about raising a child alone. She would never be alone while she chose to live around her family. Her siblings' children had given her nice practice babies to clean and cuddle and feed, and she loved them with all her heart. And through them she knew she'd be good at mothering. And her family would be good to her, helping to raise her son or daughter on the streets of the West Side of New York. And there would be a place for her uptown at Spenser International for as long as Jack breathed. Poor Jack. Did her face behind the switchboard every morning now remind him of both his young wife's early death, and his friend's? And why did she somehow believe that he had something more directly to do with Philippe's death? There were too many things that did not make sense about Spencer International. The kids thought it was a front for spies. They were reading too many comic books. Even Dick Tracy was hunting spies these days in the funny papers.

"Are you cold, *milada*?" her mother asked now.

"Stop coddling her, Ma," Anya admonished. "We finally got her out and look how much better she is. Color in her cheeks. See, you can't live at work and in your apartment, Kitty! You always loved the winter!"

Kitty pulled her hat lower, and felt that strange pain in her shoulder, the same one she'd felt that morning when reaching for a tin of oatmeal. Then. The wetness between her legs.

"Ma."

"What is it, *milada*?"

"I think I need to get home."

"Of course. We go. Anya can come along later with the children."

But they'd only reached the carriage road when the sharp pain at the abdomen doubled her over.

"Mama," she cried softly. "This can't be happening. It's too cruel." She looked behind them and saw a bright red path in the snow. She'd only meant to lean on her mother's arm, but the world tilted and she was on the ground, staring at the sky, listening to her mother's brook-no-nonsense voice hailing a cab. No, not a cab, a horse, leading a big black carriage. Inside was a formidable looking lady who was soon calling her mother "Sister Suffragette" and giving Kitty her own place in the carriage. A very warm place, lined with furs.

* * *

When she opened her eyes, her surroundings were much more antiseptic, except for the scent of a garden of cut flowers surrounding her narrow hospital bed. Her mother was there too, looking so tired. Hannah Berry's kind, deep-set eyes were shadowed and puffy, she had been crying. But it was her mother, her salt-and-pepper hued hair in the top knot she had worn since she was a factory pieceworker at the turn of the century. She wore her Sunday dress, without an apron. And behind her stood the grey-haired carriage lady in a wonderful hat, and Jack Spencer beside her.

"There, that's better," her mother said, quietly.

"Indeed it is. You have durable children, Hannah. Long may they thrive," the lady said, pressing her mother's shoulder. Jack leaned over and kissed Kitty's cheek, but said nothing before ushering the woman out.

Her mother brought her bedside chair in closer. "Your father has the rest of the family outside, just barley keeping them from busting down the door. But this is our time, first, *milada*."

"The baby's gone," Kitty began for her mother, who had suffered so much, and could be spared this. She looked down at the blankets, at her middle, which she had only imagined a small bulge of pregnancy was starting. The bandages made a larger bulge now. But she knew she was empty. She felt her mother squeeze her hand.

"Yes. And we almost lost you, too. The baby was not growing in the right place, Kitty. It was not in your womb, it was in your tube and the tube burst and well, you almost bled to death, you see? The doctor, he had to go inside you, to stop the bleeding. He had to, to take ...things out. But you're back. You're back with us, my darling, and we are so happy."

Those wounded eyes. Kitty couldn't ask, the question her mother was waiting for — The doctor took out everything, didn't he, so no more children for me, huh, Mama? So she asked another one.

"Who was that woman? The one who was so kind to us?"

"Annie?" She smiled and a spark of mischief came into her eyes. "You think you're the only one who has friends in high places,

185

daughter? Well, to tell you the truth, I am very surprised she recognized me. She's from my working girl days, that one. Joined our picket line, back when we were striking at the Triangle Factory, back before my job at Child's, and your father, and all of you. We made fun of Annie and her friends at first. Even the newspapers called them the "mink brigade" because they were rich socialites, you know, about our own age, slumming it. But she was the real thing, a reformer who went against her own people, like our president now, to help the workers. And she was right, the police didn't beat us when the ladies of high society walked the line with us. She paid many a striker's fine too, and even sued the police, imagine! Well, I figured it was only right that I join up with her and help her organize for women's suffrage, you know? When the first war came she was off to France to help the refugees and we got out of touch. But she sure came in handy in the park, didn't she? Wow, what a horse and buggy ride! And you should have seen her browbeat those doctors to take good care of you. By the time we got to St. Vincent's we had your Mr. Spenser joining her in no time. They know each other, of course,. Those doctors never had a chance against the two of them!"

The merriment left her mother's eyes. "But you do, my darling. You have a second chance now. And you will have to decide what to do with it."

Chapter 21

"*Hola mi amor.*"

What now? Luke caught the scent of heady perfume, fried potatoes, and metal. And blue skirts, reminding him of the sky. That beautiful cloudless Spanish sky, what was the name of its color? Azul. When had he last seen it? Luke lifted his head, not sure he was awake.

But there was the blue skirt, and her face, her easy, lazy smile. He searched the cell's confines. Where was Isaiah? He'd say if the woman was a dream or not.

"You didn't want to share me with a Jew, did you?" she asked, loudly.

No. He would not have dreamed of her saying that. Her mother was a Morrano, the name her enemies gave to a converted Jew who practiced in secret. His training had told him to be on the lookout for them, for they were natural possible allies. This woman's mother was dead in the bombing of Guernica. She was disparaging Isaiah Morgenstern now, but for the benefit of others, others who were listening, perhaps watching them. This must be real, Luke decided.

Her voice softened. "No chair. Shall I sit in your lap, then?"

He sat up, checked his feet. Yes, his boots were on. He looked across from him. She was still there. He nodded slowly.

She came to him, eased herself into his lap, her necklaces clicking. And a new one. Red, sparkling glass beads. Had the bribe money he'd left her on the beach bought it? He sighed deeply, breathing out the pain her weight was causing the burn wounds around his middle.

She pressed his head against breasts that were moist and scented with fear.

"There, now," she whispered. "You are only a boy, aren't you? So young, to cause them so much trouble. But never mind. I am charged to make you forget about all that." Her hands began unbuttoning his trousers. "And yes, good." She smiled for the first time. "You are happy to see your Magdalena."

Women enjoyed their power over men. The pain that Luke thought was his forever began to ease, conquered by the expertise of her hand, her whispers at his ear. "Yes. Enjoy. But quietly now, that's the way, my heart."

It was a good torment, trying to control his breathing as he gripped her waist and lost himself in waves of delight.

"I am breaking their rules," she said at his ear, "They told me to tempt only. But what do they know about the subtleties of pleasure, *mi corazón*?"

Her stroking intensified as her other hand coursed through his scalp, a holy place. Luke felt the heat rise from his core and infuse his mangled torso, his limbs. It made his legs weak. It flowed back to what she called him: her heart. This was something more than a simple, transgressive kindness. He bit into her shoulder as his body released his seed.

"Thank you, Magdalena," he whispered, licking the mark he'd left, tasting salt.

His thoughts turned again toward finding Nantai, and the open sea, and home. The woman on his lap was not being paid for this gift, this release of despair, this restoration of hope. What if they found out she'd given all of this to him? What would they do to her? He had to hide the return of his strength. He had to protect her.

She ran her bottom lip along his earlobe as she whispered. "Ah, men are such glorious, simple creatures. When you are not slaughtering each other." She took his steaming face between her hands and shook her head so that her golden earrings sang. "Now, do not look so satisfied. I have promised only, yes? Promised you may come inside me after you tell them what they want to hear.

"But the word has come to us. There is no more time, *mi corazòn*." Her whisper was now tinged with regret. "Do you understand me?"

Luke nodded, wondering what had happened to his voice.

"Good. Here, more temptations — some *pintxos* for you to enjoy. Smell them?"

He did. Potatoes, eggs, quail and fish.

He nodded again.

She didn't seem to mind his silence as she pulled the brightly embroidered cloth package from her deep pocket and placed it in his hands.

"These delights, they come from the island of Santa Clara," she chatted on. "Do you know it?"

Another nod. He remembered it form Captain Lomax's map.

"Good." She pressed her gift deeper into his hands. "Eat slowly, to remind you of the free breezes you will find there. Slowly, yes? For there are more gifts packed within."

He left his face against her heart, wanting to stay there forever, but knowing that she was directing him to action.

"You will find Santa Clara, yes? They tell me very little, but it is large enough for a landing field. And now, give your Magdalena a kiss."

She held his head locked between those fierce, strong hands, as she placed her mouth over his. An erotic mix of sex and death sparked his veins like small charges, exploding their possibilities.

When their kiss ended, she traced his eyebrow.

"There now," she announced loudly to their eavesdropping guards. "I have corrupted you enough for confession, I think, shepherd. Let us give the priest his turn to tempt what they want out of you."

And then she was gone.

Father Mikolas entered the cell. Another miracle: those steadfast, intelligent eyes, the neatly clipped beard surrounded by the linen of his cowl, the scent of his stone church and its mysteries.

Magdalena's visit was wearing off. Luke's fiery wounds flared. His head swam in confusion. He struggled to find his voice.

"Nantai?" he asked the priest. "Did you see Nantai, Father?"

The priest came closer. "They say he is too ill."

But not too ill to be set free, Luke thought. He could do it. He was strong enough to carry his clan brother out of here.

"A visit from his confessor is especially needed! The health of the soul is the higher obligation than political or military obligation,' I tell them," the priest continued. "You do not look well yourself, my son. I will write it in my report!" He said loudly, for their listeners.

Where were their listeners, Luke wondered.

"They forget they cannot inflict on Americans what they inflict on their own people," the priest shouted. "Not without the Red Cross being informed, not without international consequence! Without, perhaps, even their country's neutral status being in jeopardy!"

Did someone truly care about what these people were doing to him? Was he not the one at fault — for being too interested in life and

191

hope and finding Nantai? Too interested in these things to break the capsule between his teeth, to stop causing embarrassment to Mr. Spencer?

"My dear son. They say you should confess to them before the Germans arrive."

"Germans?"

"Just as I told them. Of what interest are you to Germans? You are a humble shepherd. Your only crime was being on a beach after curfew, a foolish American, too free, too unfamiliar with curfews." He lowered his voice to a whisper. "That's all they know with certainty. That's all they can prove. That's why they have allowed Magdelena and I to come in. In case things go in your favor, you will remember her visit, the gift of her pleasures. As for me? As usual, much less interesting. I am the gift of their own salvation. In case they kill you, they are still good Catholics, and have not sent a soul to hell without absolution…do you understand?"

Luke nodded.

"Would you like to make your confession, now that the whore has corrupted you?" he demanded loudly.

Who was Mikolas? He wanted a confession, too? Did he work for all sides?

"To your God only," the priest said, as if sensing Luke's suspicion. Father Mikolas placed his red stole around his neck. Luke knelt beside the bed, but swayed. The priest caught his arm. His voice became a charged whisper.

"Good God, what they are doing to you?" he said in a furious whisper. "How much strength do you have? Take your time, my son," he said, louder. "Did the woman tempt you with her body?"

Confession. The strange restrictions, denials of the life of the body. He would never understand the *belegaana*. No. He would not confess any part of Magdalena's visit. Find something else. Something else weighing on his heart.

"I did not row hard enough, Father Mikolas."

The priest bent over. "Luke. You are the sinned against, not the sinning." Their eyes met. "Listen to me. This much I know. Lorca the smuggler threw the explosive, as a distraction. He was afraid for his own skin, afraid of capture, because he helped some of your friends reach their boat, without asking questions. Without knowing all the connections to who he was defying. He is sorry, and has provided this gift."

Luke felt metal at his palm. A small skeleton of a firearm, but a firearm. Cool, welcome.

Lorca the smuggler, Magdalena's competitor, Luke remembered. He must have found Nantai's group, or Ingrassia's, and brought them to the beach, hoping for more reward, maybe, from the captain of the ship Varian.

"It must be tonight," Father Mikolas whispered. Once the Germans arrive, the jaws of the Third Reich will snap."

Luke pressed the firearm against the heat of his wounds, placed his waistband over it. Blessings of pleasure and food from a prostitute. The means of death from the hands of a priest.

The *belegaana* world, already crazy, was now upside down.

* * *

His captors made a mistake, Luke thought, once his priest and Magdalena had left. They returned him into the care of Isaiah Morgenstern, who they thought small and weak, of no consequence. His Kokopeli, looking more tattered than usual, yanked himself out of the grip of the guards and strode into their cell. They locked the door behind him. The guards' footsteps retreated.

The small man frowned, folding his arms.

"Visitors now, you're getting. So they make me leave our humble abode. Me, your landlord! Leave, take my life into my hands playing soccer with that great fool Telmo the Basque in the yard. What are you grinning at? This is my best shirt. Beyond repair, this sleeve! Well. Soon you'll have no time for me, with all your admirers."

How did Luke know he was teasing? The ripple over the man's scared eyebrow? The tone of voice, reminding him of the dry, deadpan

194

humor of his own people? Perhaps the Dinè were a lost tribe of Israel after all.

Very lost.

Isaiah approached his cot. "So. Who were they who came visiting? And what smells like real food in here?"

"Huh," Luke grunted. "Don't you know everything already?"

"Me? Since when am I El-Olam, the everlasting one, who knows all?"

"Who?"

"You know! Yahweh! Jehovah? Or Adonai, when he's dealing with you Gentiles. Didn't your missionaries bother with the Torah...your bible, and how to put a name to —?"

"Oh. You mean Creator?"

"Yes, yes! Except my people don't speak the Creator's name."

"How am I supposed to know that, after you just told me six of them?"

His cellmate's frown deepened. Was Isaiah stumped? Not so soon, surely. Being descended from persecuted people, they were both good at the everlasting questions game.

"No pleading ignorance," Morgenstern declared, giving up suddenly.

"Am I not ignorant? And didn't Telmo give you enough gossip without you plaguing me?" Luke tried to get started again with two questions.

"He told me some things of interest, maybe."

"What?"

Kokopelli Man looked, suddenly, sad. "First, dinner."

"No." Luke finally gave up the game. "Not first. Last. This will be our last dinner." He opened Magdalena's cloth on the floor between them. Thin wooden stakes speared pinto potato and egg omelets, and bits of cod.

"You first, oh shepherd, my shepherd."

Luke shrugged and began the careful chewing. He held out a chunk of potato to his friend with an admonition. "Eat slowly. Very slowly. And carefully."

"Why?"

"Pits."

"Pits? In fish? In these crazy latkes? Leave you for an hour with fancy, gift-giving guests and you go completely off your — ow!"

"Shouldn't talk while eating, maybe."

"What in the name of —!"

Luke opened his palm showing Isaiah the three companions of what the older man now dislodged from his mouth.

"That's four."

Bullets stuffed within the *Pintxos*.

Luke brought the smuggler's gift from his waistband. Kokopeli Man masked his delight with a displeased grunt.

"Four? So. You've been eating without me."

"You were busy gossiping on the ball field." Luke smiled. "We leave tonight."

Isaiah finally grinned in that face-halving way, expressing pure pleasure. There. Luke felt, what his friend called *mechaya koontz:* delicious accomplishment. Why was it so important to make his elder with the steel nerves smile?

Because Isaiah Morgenstern had been so good to him. And being the means toward that smile was the only gift Luke had left.

Chapter 22

Luke slept lightly, but felt himself gaining strength from the food and rest after Isaiah Morgenstern's careful tending of his burns. It still hurt, even to breathe, but it did not threaten to consume him.

He smelled strong steaming coffee and leather. Then he heard the sound of hurried footsteps advancing toward their cell.

And the diplomat's voice.

"They are coming, they are coming" he said. "Blasted Germans do not do anything at a decent hour!"

Had Isaiah eaten too much of Magdalena's bounty? His eyes were still hazy, between worlds. Luke nudged his shoulder. "Wake up, Sergeant Morgenstern. We must be soldiers now."

Luke calculated space and distance as the two targets entered their cell. The director of the prison, who had ordered Luke's burning, was the henchman for the diplomat, standing by the door. Demoted a class level, and on guard. The diplomat was not wary, he was used to being protected. And they both thought they were with weakened, demoralized victims of their abuse.

The two had only one weapon, a German Lugar, in plain sight, strapped against the director's uniform.

Were any of the diplomat's bodyguards beyond the cell door, Luke wondered. Or were they outside the building, in the courtyard,, smoking cigarettes with the chauffeur?

He sensed the soft-spoken diplomat's heart through his linen clothes, pumping hard, afraid. Not of them, though he should have been, for Luke was already targeting that heart. The diplomat was afraid of the coming Germans, he surmised. The hand that held a steaming blue crockery cup of coffee shook slightly.

It required so much energy to concentrate, to see these things clearly that Luke couldn't speak. But Isaiah was wide awake now, and could.

"My report to the International Red Cross will now include this harassment of American citizens, detained for an unconscionable period of time without benefit of counsel or the naming of charges!"

Luke tried to warn him quiet with a look. Too late. The director slammed Isaiah so hard against the wall that Luke feared it broke his neck. But Isaiah groaned and gave Luke a hapless look that said *your turn with them now.*

The diplomat sniffed, his face taking on a mildly impatient look to mask all that fear. "We have no more use for the silly Jew. Kill him," he ordered, as if he were asking for a second cup of coffee.

The commander smiled as he unlatched his firearm from its holster. Luke needed that time. Only that. To slide his own sleeve gun into his hand.

It was a single shot weapon with one round of 0.32-inch ammunition. It only gave him one chance. The cell was small, well within its three-yard range.

The commander's leather holster made a muffled squeak as the gun began to slide free.

Luke fired.

Everyone stood frozen as the coffee cup fell and shattered across the stone floor.

Luke's hand stung from holding the muzzle of his spent weapon.

The diplomat broke the spell. "Idiot!" he said. "Look what you've done, I'm burned!" He displayed his hand, splashed with hot coffee.

His words held no meaning for the commander, who crumpled to the hard stone floor, a thin line of blood trickling down between lifeless eyes.

Isaiah sprang like a cougar, so fast that Luke only heard a sharp intake of surprise before his friend and the diplomat landed on the floor beside the coffee cup remains. Kokopelli turned into cougar as Isaiah opened the jugular vein quickly, efficiently with one claw — his razor-sharp thumbnail.

He drew back. "Yours is a better death than the ones you delivered to my comrades Boland, Fisher, and Greenburg," he told his prey, who could only make a gurgling sound as death claimed his body.

Isaiah Morgenstern wiped his thumb on the man's still-immaculate linen vest.

"Thank you, my friend," he said, this day is starting off in a most promising manner. And we still have hours before dawn." He moved to dislodge the Lugar from the dead prison director's hand. "Reload that pea shooter, Bunkie, while I see if —" he turned the body over, "yes, our unlamented tormentor comes with a complement of keys. And no one is coming to their rescue...they were told to expect gunshots, if my demise was always in their plan, I imagine. Well, shall we do your Americans one better? Shall we offer this hell hole full liberation?"

"Why not?" Luke agreed, realizing he was still playing Isaiah's questions game, though the tone of their voices was now more grim. He shoved the napkin filled with the rest of Magdalena's bullets into his pocket. "You can have the liberating pleasure. I'm going to the infirmary for Nantai."

"No. Luke. Listen to me. We need to begin liberation, then meet with Telmo, first."

"Telmo?"

"Telmo the Basque. He can help us to find your friend. Please. Trust me."

Luke felt darkness encircling his heart, but nodded. All right," he said.

Luke knew the way to all the cells now, even better than Isaiah did. He led the way, as they heard the sounds of increasing chaos above their heads. These were desperate, determined men. They had survived years in this place. They knew where the firearms were. They had pre-dawn darkness and surprise on their side. They might succeed, or, as Isaiah said, "die trying."

When they arrived at his cell, Luke did not like the look in Telmo's eyes.

"*Si*. I know where the other shepherd is."

Isaiah frowned. "Well? What do you want in exchange?" he demanded.

"A weapon," the burly man replied.

Isaiah dug into his waistband, handed over the German Lugar he'd retrieved from the commander's body.

Telmo checked its ammunition load. "He is with the crusader."

"What are you saying?"

Telmo held up one hand, while the other guarded his new weapon.

"I carried him there myself. He was a light burden."

"Will you show us the way?" Isaiah asked quietly.

Telmo sighed hard. "Yes, if you give Martinez the remaining keys, allow him to complete our liberation."

Isaiah turned to Telmo's cellmate, a Basque with haunted eyes. "Here. Remember. Open them all," he instructed.

Telmo led the way with an oil lantern he'd grabbed from another fleeing prisoner. Luke felt the air get closer, more dense. Stairs, in a circle, forever downward. Distant, muffled blasts. Gunshots? The fight for liberation had begun. Along a corridor. Down more stairs that he did not count. He couldn't keep numbers in his head any more.

The last door opened soundlessly. Dry, cool. A domed room, larger, longer than Luke's torture room. It still had its ancient frescoed walls, full of vibrant color and stories. Telmo stood in the doorway,.

Luke looked deeply into his Kokopeli's eyes as he raised the lamp higher. Isaiah's face was kind, for all its traces of fierce cougar.

"My dear *shepseleh*, I wasn't sure this was real," he said as they both stared in wonder at their surroundings. The frescoes on the ceiling's arches pictured plants and animals painted in brilliant colors and infused with gold and lapis lazuli. They framed scenes of draped people holding babies, celebrating with wine and with angels, meeting on hilltops, escaping the Great Flood, and the Pharaoh of Egypt.

"The prisoners, they talk about this place," Isaiah continued, "dating from the time of Queen Sancha of Castile. And about this warrior, a Crusader of the wars they call holy. He's been preserved here because of the dryness. Feel it?"

Luke nodded, confused, barely able to keep up with Isaiah Morgenstern's rapid-fire speech.

"I knew you wouldn't leave here without knowing. Luke, your friend Nantai is dead, and there's nothing you can do, except live for him."

"Dead?"

Was that his voice, so young, so lost?

Telmo spoke good Spanish, with an accent from his own first language, a language Luke had heard during his times in the village below the mountain. It was wonderful and strange and like nothing he'd ever heard before. Telmo's Basque-accented Spanish was slow, deliberate, as if he was talking to a child, or in a ritual.

"I was on clean-up duty the night they brought you in. You, my friend, went into the commander's rooms. Your friend was pulled out of the vehicle, put on the ground. They were complaining that you were still blacked-out and he had told them nothing. But he was babbling about a gorilla, so they thought he'd like to see the prisoner who looked most like an ape. They think themselves so clever, so amusing. But when he saw me he smiled, you know? As if he were being united with a long-lost brother. This made them furious, and they demanded to know his name. 'Monster Slayer' he told them.

"That made them more angry. They loosened the belt tied tight around his leg. The blood. I have never seen so much blood. And them, laughing, they were laughing, watching him die. Your friend, he took my hand then, comforting me. Can you imagine that? Comforting me as his life blood left his body. 'I walk in beauty,' he said. And that was the end

204

on him. I took care of his body. I took good care of him, I can assure you, sir. And they told me to bring him here, and not speak of that night, or the man they had killed, for their own sport, under pain of death. I am sorry for the loss of Monster Slayer. I would have liked to know him."

Luke felt Telmo's big, gnarled hand grip his shoulder, then release it. He spoke to Isaiah.

"Can you find your way back, Morgenstern?"

"Yes, my friend. And thank you, from us both."

"I will be going, then. May we meet again in better times." The big man transferred the lamp to Isaiah's hand.

Luke forced his eyes to follow its light.

The first being the light found was shriveled within his armor. Not the armor of the Conquistadors, but an earlier, more graceful kind, meant to shield from spears and arrows, not gunpowder. This was a man his ancestors would have been glad to meet in battle, on equal terms. The body had been there a long time, so long that Luke's instinctual fear of the dead was gone. The man had become something more permanent, almost part of an elaborately carved stone bed, full of spirals and interlocking circles. He seemed a powerful stone sentinel himself, guarding his much newer guest.

The guest was on the small wooden pallet in the Crusader's shadow.

Isaiah approached with the lamp. Luke followed.

Nantai was swaddled in white, with a slight yellow tinge to his skin. Luke had a sudden vision of him in his cradleboard, hanging from a low juniper tree. Perhaps it was his expression, full of a newborn's peace.

Nantai had left his silver and turquoise jewelry with the women. There was nothing to mark him Dinè in this place, this strange, beautiful place, echoing centuries of cruelty, so far from home.

But a holy place. And Nantai had a powerful guardian, one who would not fail him.

Luke knelt. He touched his clan brother's shoulder.

"Did I hear you singing from here?" he whispered.

Isaiah approached. "No, my friend. From here."

He touched the aching place over Luke's heart.

"We need to go now."

Luke nodded, rose, fighting the deep desire to lie down beside his brother and the ancient warrior, to rest from the madness above ground.

Perhaps the Dinè taboos against touching the dead were not about disease and infection but about this longing to join them, Luke thought.

Chapter 23

Luke and Isaiah found the above world was in chaos. The guards' organization and firepower were winning over any advantage the prisoner's surprise actions may have had. Still, pockets of the oppressed had stolen weapons, were covering each other, and looking for ways out. But others were terrified, running, going down.

Telmo, leading five men, two of them bleeding, gathered around Luke and Isaiah.

"Ammunition?" Isaiah barked.

"Out."

The others held up rocks. Luke took stock of their present arsenal. Two confiscated Lugars awaiting reloading, his almost useless close range sleeve gun with its few bullets, and rocks.

He scanned the courtyard and sensed more fear, not from their enlarging company, but from within the heavy car of the diplomat. The vehicle was riddled with bullets. None appeared to have pierced its surface. Armored, then. He thought of the code Dinè word Nantai had suggested for armored vehicles: Turtle Back.

Luke leaned toward Isaiah. "We need more arms."

"Agreed."

"We could get them at the guardhouse."

"How?"

Luke nodded toward the automobile. "The driver is under the front seat."

"How do you know that?"

"His red coattail, there, caught. See?"

"No. But I'll trust your younger eyes."

"We break the window, pull him out, get the keys. The vehicle is ours."

Three others joined their gathering, heard the plan.

"Cover us?" Luke asked.

Several grinned, holding up their rocks. One revealed a lead pipe.

"If we make it, climb on the runner boards, stay low," Luke told them. "We are heading for the guardhouse for rearming."

Telmo nodded, his black eyes bright with hope.

* * *

Helmut Adler rolled down the limousine's window as the countryside sped by. Where had the Spanish gotten a comfortable 1940 Packard Super 8? Probably confiscated it from a rich American tourist traveling the countryside, oblivious to the civil unrest that plagued this backward peninsular.

The switch-backed roads enabled them to climb higher. The air smelled like that of the Great American Plains. He remembered how the high desert of his boyhood adventure novel dreams came to searing life during his expeditions in the American West.

Desolate, drought-scourged fields. Dust Bowl, the Americans called it then. It was desolate, almost empty of human habitation, left for the bone picking paleontologists like himself.

If his bleary-eyed driver had not lost his way from the air field, he would not be picking the bones of his past missions to the United States. He would be picking the brains of the two American Indians. That is, if they'd left him any live prey, in the Spanish pit of a prison. Had they?

Adler didn't like the extra measure of calm that had permeated the diplomat's voice over the phone lines. What did it hide? Why wasn't he at the air field himself? Where was he? He'd left only the car and driver, with directions on their journey to the prison. *Zur Hölle mit der hinterlader!* Did the Spanish queer proceed to the prison ahead of him? Without a doubt. Why? To put a clean face on the mess they'd made? Or to crow over getting a confession first?

Adler didn't like either possibility. He growled out his frustration.

His driver twitched. Adler rolled his window up. He liked the way his swastika-emblazoned armband alone was enough to strike a kind of hunted fear into these Spaniards.

Adler forced himself to breathe more slowly. And plan.

In his decade of wanderings, he had found Americans resourceful, for all the sloppiness of their undisciplined lives. He expected these two to survive the beginnings of the blunt torture of the Spanish. But they'd already hinted one was severely injured.

The Spanish would not have killed their prisoners, not once they heard that his orders were from Himmler himself. They would not have dared.

Perhaps the Americans would even be weakened enough to make his treatments work faster. He'd brought an arsenal of the latest injections. They would render that language, and the code within it. Quickly. Efficiently. Scientifically.

Let the Spanish deal with the diplomatic consequences. He was above such details.

His country was at war. It had been, to Adler's way of thinking, since the guns began firing in August, 1914. The humiliations of their so-called peace of twenty years ago would be avenged.

The car's speed began to decrease. Adler leaned forward. "Driver. What is going on?"

The driver's attention remained on the road.

"Another car, sir. A consulate car, coming from the other direction."

It was true then. The diplomat had awoken from his beauty rest to head for the prison before him.

Adler smiled. Good.

"Move to the center of the road. Do not let it pass. Perhaps the consulate's auto is even more comfortable than this one. And German made. Perhaps the great man will exchange vehicles with his guest."

"I think the auto has had better days, sir."

"What are you talking about?"

But in the glare of the headlights, he was already catching glimpses of damage to the Mercedes-Benz 770. A crushed fender, broken windows, bullet holes. The vehicle came to a stiff-braked halt only inches from his car's own headlights.

One door opened with a punishing crack at its hinges. Two officers, one as burly as an ape, the other as slight as a woman, advanced towards his car.

Much more quietly, a tall chauffeur slipped from the driver's side. He stood, almost blending into the night, his hat low over his eyes. All the uniforms were scorched and dirty, but the chauffeur filled his with a calm menace that kept Adler's attention riveted.

Was this man targeting him? Every instinct was proclaiming that he was.

The slight officer bowed curtly. "If you would please let us by," he said.

Adler signaled for his driver to speak. "This is a German envoy," the man began nervously.

The slight officer bowed again, in his direction this time, but somehow without the deference that Adler both expected and despised.

And, another surprise. The man's language switched to good, if Bavarian-tainted, German. "There has been an uprising at the prison, your excellence. This road is not safe."

Adler smiled. "Then it will be your duty to keep us safe."

"We are loaded with our wounded, and are ordered——"

"What of the American survivors of the escape off Zurriola beach?"

A pause. Slight. The ape man shifted his weight to his other foot. The tall chauffeur remained motionless. Except for his eyes, which narrowed. Moaning sounded from inside the battered car.

"Ah. Of course, the Americans," the small officer said evenly. "Our esteemed Consul stays on at the prison, with his elite force, personally protecting the Americans from the uprising. We are sent to leave off the wounded at hospital, then gather reinforcements. Perhaps you would desire to follow us to San Sebastian and," the slightest pause, "out of harm's way?"

There was a quirt of challenge in the small, scarred officer's pause. A veteran, this was. The arrogance of these backwoods Spaniards, to question his courage.

Adler looked again to the diplomat's chauffeur. The dark, undoubtedly Moorish or other mongrel Spanish face was bruised. Adler somehow felt sure that those who had caused his pain were now dead.

Adler faced the two officers. "We will advance to the prison, of course. Render what assistance we can."

"Well. As you wish, sir."

Only when Adler had given his own driver the order to move aside and allow the diplomat's car to pass, did that chauffeur re-enter the consulate car. Adler caught a closer glimpse of the high plane of the man's face as their automobiles passed each other. A glint of blood shone, disappearing into his maroon uniform's collar. Someone else's blood.

The chauffeur was a warrior. The damned diplomat had taken the best man for his own staff, his own protection, of course.

Chapter 24

Luke felt the charge of energy bleed out of him as he slid back behind the wheel.

"I wanted to kill him," he said, quietly.

Isaiah Morgenstern granted him a rueful smile. "Thank you for not acting on your desire, Lieutenant. We must try our wits first, whenever we can. Oppressed people, like yours and mine, have always known this, yes?"

Telmo and his several of his compatriots, who were piled onto the floor and backseat of the limousine, snorted.

"Good moaning, men," Isiah complimented them.

They drove until the car ran out of fuel from its leaking gas tank. Then the men got out and pushed it into the brush.

Telmo stepped forward, slinging a rifle to his shoulder. His comrades stood behind him.

"We make our way deeper into the mountains. We know how to disappear. You are welcome in our company."

Luke liked the idea of disappearing. But Isaiah answered. "And spend the rest of my life trying to understand Basque? When on Orchard Street my father's shop may be looking for a good watch fixer?" he teased his old nemesis.

Telmo laughed. "You're making a mistake, old man. Our women are the best lovers. They like even ancient Americans. And this one," he his chin pointed toward Luke, "he will have no peace. Even with a coat which will scarcely keep his and his lover's back from the cold of these mountains!"

They continued insulting each other, but their words became harder for Luke to translate. Were they talking too fast? The world seemed to be moving out of his senses' control.

"Why, look what is left of his coattails!"

The men joined in Telmo's laugher. Why?

Luke looked down. Under his arm and along the back of the chauffeur's uniform, only the lining was left, the cold breeze fanning its tatters. When had that happened? Was it after he'd pulled the driver onto the running board and seen the glint of the man's knife? How was he in the man's clothes? He couldn't remember.

Did he still have his boots on? Yes. They were important, something to do with the airman's wife. He would remember, if he could just close his eyes.

Telmo laughed again. "Morgenstern! Your man is asleep on his feet!"

"There's strength left in him." Isaiah countered.

Luke grunted, making them all laugh again.

Remember. Remember what to say to this man who did a great service for Nantai. "Thank you, for taking care of my clan brother. You have honored us. You have honored Dinetah."

Telmo's eyes grew sad. Then he slapped Luke's back, before he and his men disappeared over a ridge.

The air was colder without them.

Luke leaned on a rock outgrowth that reminded him of Turtle, in the stories, and the way to find the airman's grave.

The small man took hold of Luke's arm. "Look at me!" he commanded. "It's all down hill from here. You see that ocean? America's on the other side of it, my friend, my dear *shepseleh*. America."

Luke saw only the women standing outside their hogan wailing for Nantai, and he did not want to go home.

But Isaiah Morgenstern's shoulder was under his arm, boney and insistent.

"You think your people will take me without you? Not on your life! Who am I to them? A leftie rabble-rouser, a Russian Jew's immigrant son, who went to fight a war that was none of my business. Who wants me? Nobody! But their shepherd, my dear *shepseleh*, my *tateleh*, my bunkie, he's a different story. I don't know why. I don't want to know why. Now, how can I bribe you to take the next step?"

"Peaches."

"Peaches," he repeated.

"Yes. Fresh. Ripe."

"You're worse than Telmo, that thief, with your demands! Where am I going to find peaches?"

"Don't you live on Orchard Street?"

"Have you ever been to the Lower East side of New York, rube?"

"Flew over it once." The memory shot strength to his limbs. "I like flying."

Luke had a vague sense of being tricked, by a language full of questions and interesting pictures, tricked to stay on his feet, tricked into moving, so that he could find out what would happen next in Isaiah Morgenstern's world of words.

Spencer found that interesting, the words of Luke's language. He enjoyed turning Dinè words back into English, forming a code talk for radioed messages. A game that he and Nantai practiced, while watching the sheep in the hills of this country, an ocean away. Practiced so well that it took only seconds to decode messages. He had done that much, he had guarded the secret of their game, even from his friend Isaiah Morgenstern.

How would Spencer know that the secret was still safe? Nantai had not betrayed the code. On the beach. Luke remembered now, their flight, the explosion, the gushing of his clanbrother's heart blood. He remembered what the men had been saying around him as he struggled under Nantai's weight...

"This one will not survive. Have a care with the other."

Nantai was dead. Telmo had been there, witnessed his bravery as they let him die. He had died talking about King Kong, not giving up the code, not giving them anything. Then, these

Spanish, they had only used Luke's belief that it was not so, that Nantai lived. Used it to get what they wanted, for themselves, for the Germans. For the man who watched him from the auto with hatred in his eyes. Nantai was dead, in the Crusader's beautiful tomb. What of his leg? Had they left it on the beach? *Stop it.* They were soldiers. Such things were not their business. And what could he do about anything, now? He himself was growing more useless by the moment. Who would tell Jack Spencer that there was no betrayal, that the code was safe?

"Luke!" Isaiah summoned his eyes open again. "Do you know where we should go?"

"Santa Clara."

"The island?"

"Yes."

"But they'll never get a ship close enough to pick us up there."

"Santa Clara," he repeated, trusting Magdalena's words, her own sly code, given along with his pleasure.

Isaiah Morgenstern sighed. "All right, bunkie. Santa Clara it is."

* * *

The clouds obscured the moon and stars. Good weather for making their way around the north side of San Sebastian, but bad for celestial navigation.

The beach on this more remote side of the town was not long and white and curved, but

218

dark, dense-packed and rocky. Luke was grateful for the difference. Something to concentrate on, something to keep the memory of Nantai's blood away.

Still, when they were standing on this different beach, Luke hesitated, staring down at the small boat. He saw Nantai, on white sand, chiding him for his slowness. Nantai had been doing that since their childhood together, because Luke was always taller, broader, and older by one changing of the moon.

"Come," another man called him from the boat now. Isaiah. His Kokopelli.

He and Isaiah began to maneuver the craft together. He saw worry invade Isaiah's eyes. Could he see Luke's heartsickness? His grief? He tried to grunt it away from himself.

"Put your whole body's force behind the pushing," Luke advised, "not your arms."

Isaiah nodded curtly and pressed his lips together for their next haul over the rocks. How unnaturally silence hung on his Kokopelli, Luke thought.

Once in the boat and on the water, Isaiah gestured toward Luke's shirt and its fresh red stains. "Look what you're doing to my nice fix-it job."

"It doesn't matter."

"Of course it matters, they'll think I didn't take good care of you. They'll feed me to some German U-boat. How long would I last then?"

"Long enough to talk them to death?"

The burst of machine gun fire startled him, a long burst sending a slice of the boat's wood splintering into Isaiah Morgenstern's arm.

Luke felt a warm spray at his face. He blinked. Isaiah came into focus again.

"Heads down, row harder," Luke said quietly.

"Where?"

"Away. We have been betrayed, I think."

The shooters on Santa Clara island had not waited long enough to keep them in range.

Luke remembered the history lesson at his missionary school, and one of the few stories he liked, of another battle. "Don't fire until you see the whites of their eyes," the American had commanded at Bunker Hill.

These ones had not waited that long. They could have had them, if they had waited.

In the time the shooters took to reload the machine gun, he and Isaiah rowed out of range, and were heading for open water.

Luke ripped a strip of his chauffeur coat's lining.

"What are you doing? Pull that damned splinter out," Isaiah said.

"Better not to. It is deep. I'm sorry. I will try to keep it stable, so it won't hurt any worse." He wrapped above and below the wound tightly.

"All right. All right, doctor."

"Emergency medicine only. But my teacher was a doctor, from Scotland."

"Useful training for America's officers, now? Uncle Sam may be wising up, and none

220

too soon. There's hope for winning this war with these crazy Nazis maybe."

Isaiah's good hand probed the side of Luke's face.

"Only my blood spritzed you," he determined. "You're all right. Just me, this time. That's good."

"It is not good," Luke groused. "I'm supposed to be rescuing you."

The boat was taking on water.

Perhaps they had only been able to choose the way of their own deaths. But that was enough to send strength to Luke's limbs as he rowed.

He wondered who had sent the gunmen to the island, and if Magdalena was safe, and Father Mikolas.

He looked up from their task. Isaiah Morgenstern's eyes were losing the hope that Luke thought lived there.

"What do we do?" he asked quietly.

"Bail. And row. And wait for the moon."

A cloud moved.

The three quarter moon appeared. Its light threw the odd creature flying below it into silhouette. Then, the sound of the friendly aircraft, not the whine of a German one. Isaiah spotted it, too.

"Such service, Lieutenant! You must be some important guy."

Chapter 25

"Signal that plane away from the island, away from the guns," Luke commanded. "It must not land there."

"Now, bunkie. You should be more hospitable!"

Luke looked down. Isaiah's side of the boat was swamping as he stood, grinning at the sky.

"Send the plane away!" Luke shouted, dropping the oars.

"Hey, you can't order me, we're not in the same army!"

Luke closed his eyes against the cold, against his terror of the rising water. Against the possibility of causing more death, to the ones who had come for them.

Clouds were again closing in.

Shots peppered out from the island.

No sound of a crash.

Go away, Luke thought at the fogged-over sky, the fog-shrouded sea, *you can't save us*.

No sound at all. Had the strange looking airplane left, then? The cold water reached up to his shins. How long would the messages, wrapped in oil cloth and embedded in his boots, survive?

"Sergeant Morgenstern," he said, "I can't swim. I can barely float."

The familiar snort. "And you think I spent my summers on Brighton Beach getting a nice sun tan only? Lie back and take a breath."

"But —"

"If you please, Lieutenant, sir," Isaiah spat out. "No more arguing! Sir. Fine time you decide to pull rank, I got to tell you."

As they were swamped completely, Luke did as he was told. The wooden rowboat descended below them, and then disappeared into the cold darkness. So quietly.

Luke felt Isaiah's arm, the bandaged one, cross his chest.

"Just breathe," Isaiah whispered, there at his ear.

The sound of the plane returning. More shots from the island. Splashing, silence. Luke wished the stars would come out before the sea swallowed them. He would like to see the stars.

A wave washed over them. Luke gagged on the salty water. He heard Isaiah's breathing shorten, saw frosty gasps. He should help, kick. But he couldn't feel his legs.

Then, the flash of hands, hands with long beautiful fingers, their nails the color of azalea blossoms. Those hands closed in a grip on his shirt, and then hauled him up while Isaiah pushed.

"*Ange Lumiere*! How do you like our flying duck?" Isabelle Marius asked.

Her husband grumbled something from the pilot's seat that made her sigh.

"*D'accord, alle!*" she said over her shoulder before concentrating on Luke again. "There will be no end to Alain's arrogance, now that this man of mine, in his new toy, can land on water like the Son of God himself!"

She gifted Isaiah with a slow wink. "We know our lieutenant's habit of taking in strays, sir. You are most welcome."

"I am the most fortunate of men, tonight, Madame."

"And the other, the shepherd with few words and kind eyes?" she whispered.

"He did not survive."

"May he know the face of God."

That gleaming smile flashed, for them both. "Tuck in your wings, *Ange*. If your friend weighs less than one of the two depth charges we left behind in Scotland, we should rise into the air well enough."

As if commanded, the strange aircraft lifted over the water.

Isabelle's exotic fingers began peeling off his clothing. "Alain is very busy at the controls. So, it falls to me to keep our dear guests warm. This you would like, gentlemen?"

Her laughter chimed like the bells on his sisters' fancy dance dresses, even over the engine's roar.

Chapter 26

The Scottish Highlands

At first it had reminded Luke of the Spanish prison. The building was once a fortress, made of stone, and full of old terrors. But the air was colder, wetter. A different place, redeemed by healing, and women in white.

Isabelle drifted in like an exotic bird among the nurses. She sat beside him, parting and re-parting his hair, singing *Lilli Marlen* at his ear, in four languages, now. She told him of Magdelena, who was one of theirs, as well as a smuggler and sometime lover of loose-lipped Spanish and German officials. She told him of Magdelena's courage in getting the location of their rescue rendezvous spot to him while he was in Porta Coeli. She was a woman who made her murdered mother proud in her resistance. And it was not she who betrayed their original meeting place on Santa Clara. It was the powerful German, who could empty U-Boats of gunner crews, and post them on every island large enough for a plane to land. They all had to remain on guard for that one, known as Helmut Adler.

"But they did not provide enough guns to prevent a water landing *vis a vis* our marvelous Breguet 790 Nautilus! Though, to speak the truth, it was very clever of you to stay out of the guns' range, as our seaplane's hull is metal, but our wings are wrapped in fabric only!"

Isabelle brought sweets for the nurses and chased away Spencer's men, the ones in grey suits. They were full of questions. Important questions, they said.

Luke could not gather the strength, or find the voice to answer them. At first he could barely breathe through the shattered glass he felt his lungs had become.

A cloud descended over his spirit. It had stolen his voice, stolen words in any language.

All of his rescuers, Isaiah Morgenstern, Isabelle and Alain Marius, argued with Jack Spencer's men about his lost voice.

"He must tell us —"

"He is trying to get over the pneumonia," Isabelle insisted. Her husband took up her cause, "Which he got in your service, along with the scars."

"We have to debrief him!"

"Let him rest, gentlemen."

"We have to ask —"

"You know this man!" Isaiah proclaimed. "You know what he's done. Let him heal, get him home. Then he'll answer all your questions."

"The doctors can find nothing wrong with his voice. Why won't he —"

"Maybe it's you."

"Us?"

"He needs to see your boss, maybe."

* * *

Luke opened his eyes on another day, after roaming the Spanish mountains, looking for the place he'd buried the airman in his dreams. Isaiah Morgenstern sat beside his bed.

"Got in to see you early today, bunkie. Why? Because I'm nice to nurses, including that past-the-first-blush-of-maidenhood battle-axe one, MacArdle, who's taken a secret liking to you. Your boss Spencer's fancy swells could learn a few things from me. About how to treat the womenfolk, you know?"

Luke did know. Nurse MacArdle had little tolerance for any of his visitors except for his Kokopelli.

"I thought the Lincoln Brigade was an irregular unit," Isaiah continued. "Your bunch has got us beat, Lieutenant. Plaguing me, like I'm going home to tell Abie the fishmonger all your secrets. Secrets, which I, of course, don't know in the first place, on account of all I ever got out of you was name and rank."

He'd gotten more than that, Luke thought. But he had earned the knowledge of every word, story, detail. He would trust the small, rugged Jewish man with his life. And he would invite him into the most sacred Navajo space. He would find the best singer for his friend's

Enemyway ceremony. He would even allow Isaiah Morgenstern to court his mother, should they ever take a liking to each other.

Traveling clothes, a suit. Isaiah was going home away, Luke realized, leaving him behind. The small man who had been so good to him shifted his glance toward the stone floor.

"The medicine your boss sent for, from that moldy cantaloupe in Peoria is helping you, yeah?"

Penicillin, Luke remembered its name. *Respond. Nod. Did I? Yes. A smile from his friend.*

"Well, pull through the last of this *shreklekh* Scottish winter and you owe your life to a rotten piece of fruit. Don't know how you're going to face the future knowing that."

Trickster. Kokopelli, making a joke.

Isaiah placed his right hand over Luke's still, folded ones. His voice hushed. "*Mishpacha*, listen to me. I gotta get home now, on account of my father's sick. I'd stay until you're feeling better, if it weren't for that, you understand?"

Yes. Of course. Yes.

"Yeah, it's all right, bunkie. I know you understand honoring ancestors. We are of related people, that's why I call you this new Yiddish endearment, *Mishpacha*. It means you are like family. You like that one, bunkie?"

Yes.

Sure you do. Listen. I cleaned up your pocket watch. Got it running good. Battle Axe

MacArdle promises to wind it every morning. It gives you any trouble, or needs a cleaning, drop by the shop on Orchard Street. Will you do that, *meyn bagleyter*?"

Luke nodded.

His friend grinned as if he were in the company of a better example of what he'd called him — companion. He would never forget his kokopelli's beautiful. pieced-back-together face, his wide snaggle-toothed smile

"I wouldn't let them throw out your boots, either. I remember how touchy you were about those, bunkie. I re-blocked them nice and shined them up. Good leather. Rubber soles. Hold onto them. They'll get you home."

Isaiah pressed their joined hands.

Luke enjoyed the full silence between them.

"Ah," his friend broke it, glancing up and raising his voice. "The beauty queen of the MacArdle clan's on shift, ready to fluff your pillows, you most fortunate of men!"

"And that's more care than bloody, badgering Yanks can do fer him!" The woman sent her barbed voice out like a weapon.

Isaiah finally took his last leave of Luke's company once Stones-in-Her-Throat was there. No, not Stones-In-Her-Throat. MacArdle, Luke remembered what Isaiah had called her. Nurse MacArdle. She reminded him of his mother, although Ada Kayenta's anger sounded more like the screech of a soaring red hawk.

She was built almost as wide as his mother was tall and lean. Her hair was not neatly bound in wool, but its tight, silver curls shot out around her head and nurse's cap like crazy coils. One of her beautiful grey eyes was always looking at her own nose.

She was right about his visitors. They couldn't restore his voice, or his spirit.

He needed a ceremony, under the clear skies of home. He closed his eyes.

"Nae, now, Captain. Enough with your layin' about like a big store dog."

She piled the pillows behind his head and shoulders. How had he become a captain? Oh, yes. "Battlefield commission" one of Spencer's men said, after he'd led some of Lomax's men.

Nurse MacArdle came closer.

Perfume. Almost covering the iodine scent of her. Jack Spencer's perfume. His superior's men gave gifts to all the hospital staff. Which of the Spencer scents was hers? Luke couldn't remember a single one, and they were part of his cover story. But he'd always had the most trouble with that part of his cover, working for a man who'd made his fortune selling perfume. Knowing what a man who had that job would know.

"Din'na care for a one of yer friends from New York, except fer that last one, no matter the quality their bribes," Nurse MacArdle complained as she laid out her elaborate system of linens with her fine, freckled hands. "Spoiled. Bloody handsome, spoiled Yanks, like me mam warned me against when they came over to tea during the last war, yer visitors are, to be sure.

230

"Now hark at me, young one," she summoned, keeping her good eye on his face as her linens only exposed the part of him her hands found, cleaned, treated with her comforting ointments. "They may have flown in their fancy powder concoction from the States to cure ye, but it was Alexander Fleming of Lochfield, Ayr who first figured what penicillin might do for those suffering from congested lung, back in '28. Scratch any Yank or Englishman of worth ye'll find a Scot!"

She gave her attention to each wound as her words continued gargling like a river over stones. "Not that ye haven't earned the health returning to you, lad. The wee feller that's just now left, he with the face that's worn out three bodies? He said you got a mighty number of good folk free o' that dreadful prison."

Luke turned his face to the grey stone wall. But there was no hiding from a listening woman. And she listened well to the words he did not say. Luke's peripheral vision caught her signaling for a steaming bowl from another nurse's food cart.

Luke smelled the thin soup. He winced, prompting her hardest-stones voice.

"Turning as fussy about our food as your Frenchie friends on me, then?" She lifted the bowl from the tray and chose her weapon.

He raised his fingers. Could he show her before —

There. She stopped, hovered, put down the spoon.

"Ach, lad, easy," she said softly, the rocks becoming smooth stones. "Is it the sores around your mouth troubles ye? Shall we try a syringe, then?"

Luke felt the blood leave his face.

She sighed. "Aimed in your mouth, not your veins, lad."

He let his breath out.

"Aye, then?"

He nodded slowly.

She loaded a syringe and slipped it between his lips. The broth trickled down his throat.

He didn't cough it back up, which must have pleased her, because her shoulders lost their at-the-ready stance.

He kept swallowing.

"Good, then," she said when the bowl was empty. "Something nourishing in you, at long last."

She pressed her hands to her knees and rose to see to the needs of others. He felt her return just as he was drifting off to sleep, and without the energy to raise his eyelids.

Her fingers sifted through his hair to make room for the press of her lips on his forehead.

It was something his mother might have done, after he'd accomplished something that pleased her. Waiting, like this woman, until she thought he was asleep, so that he would not grow too boastful of her love.

* * *

232

When he woke again Nurse MacArdle was approaching his bed, sweeping off a dark blue cape. Under her perfume, it smelled of the promise of spring. "Captain, look ye here. My brother Ian sends a present."

Her hand disappeared into her pocket. "As if we are needing another stinking concoction around here! But he says it will help your mouth heal." She opened a small tin.

Luke smelled home.

"Why, laddie," she entreated, "what is it? Something hurts? Captain? Come now, show me where."

He shook his head, feeling foolish.

"Shall I call over a doctor, then?"

He shook his head harder.

She found her handkerchief and blotted his tears. She smiled sadly. "Ach now, you can tell me. Do you nae tell me everything?" she teased.

He lifted his hand toward the gift. It shook, but he didn't have to hide the shaking from her. Her eyes, as grey as the stone walls of the hospital, widened, even the one that only pointed inward.

"It's the sheep grease gone made you all sentimental? How is that?" Two fingers touched her cheek. "Wait now, those big Yanks, they called you the shepherd. I thought they were casting you in a holy light, you know, for your rescuing, comparing you to our dear Lord. Is that what you were, then? Back in the wild American West? You're a shepherd are ye, then?"

He smiled, smearing the grease across his lips.

She sat back, watching, grinning, before her no-nonsense voice returned. "Well, you'd best get yourself out of this bed, and soon. My brother will need an extra hand come shearing time."

Luke smelled home and spring though the hospital scents, and through all the centuries of black powder warfare, fire, ritual and feasting behind it in this ancient place that Nurse MacArdle called "the Keep."

Over the next days Nurse MacArdle told him where her brother's sheep station was, even mapping the way that her stout legs peddled the four miles distance, all within her stories of the sheep men going off to war, some lost at Dunkirk and others, many others shot down out of the skies as Philippe Charente had been.

* * *

Luke's bruises turned yellow except around the burns and cuts, which were still red.

He needed to be of use.

So, finally, when he judged it to be a good day, he got up while it was still dark and the night nurse asleep in the far corner of the ward.

He put on the clothes Isabelle and Alain had left in the wooden chest at the foot of his bed. He laced up boots made fine again by Isaiah, and took his grandfather's watch from its drawer, wound it, and placed it in the pocket over his heart.

He eased himself out the window and landed in small low-growing flowers, shielding themselves from the hearty wind. He did not know their names but one looked like owl's clover which bloomed in the mountains of his home, and another resembled heart leaf arnica.

He crossed the gray wool scarf around his chest, which no longer rattled when he breathed. And then, how to find his way? He would remember it from her stories.

As he rounded the third hill, the sun rose, glinting off the brook's rushing water. He thought he heard a child crying.

Then he knew better. An abandoned spring lamb was caught, washed to the center patch of earth, on a branch of thorny briar.

Cold rushing water ran over the distressed creature, but the water was not deep. And the rushing brook would be of no danger to Luke, not unless he stumbled. He was stronger now, after walking the hospital grounds every day. He would not stumble. Still, he hesitated, and felt the sweat bead his brow, the short breaths constrict his lungs. He scanned the countryside around him. No one was coming for the animal.

The lamb's struggle caught it further in the briar's grip. The cries grew weaker. The brook, though high flowing, was not an ocean.

Not an ocean, ready to take him down.

Luke yanked off his boots and coat and waded in. The lamb's face was a mix of black

235

and white, like the badger face pattern on some of the churros at home. He held out his arms, trying to keep calm, not to frighten the animal. He wished he could find a song, or a voice to sing it.

The lamb allowed him, even without a voice, to remove her from the tangle. To take on her weight, heavier than it should have been. No, it was he who was weaker. She clung when he reached the shore again.

So he carried her toward the smoke rising over a hill, though he couldn't do it without resting twice to capture his strength and breath. On the hill he heard the singing voices of children.

> *Who'd be a king, can any tell*
> *When a shepherd lives so well*
> *Lives so well and pays his due*
> *With honest heart and tarry wool.*

He felt lighter at the sound of their voices. Lighter, not so anchored in the boots and their promise to the airman Philippe Charente, still not kept.

Children's voices had always made him feel like that, he realized now. So many things he was learning in his silent time, even things he should have always known.

Suddenly, he wanted to give thanks for this revelation, here at daybreak, where he had not said his Dinè prayers for a long time.

He held the soft lamb closer, feeling the thrumming of her heart against his own. He faced the east. He closed his eyes. The sun warmed his lids.

And he waited for words. To his astonishment, they came in song. In the Dinè language, the one he heard in his mother's womb, the one the matrons and teachers tried to soap from his mind, the one his country now wanted to use to help save the world from the grip of tyranny.

Father, the Sun,
Shine brightly upon her path this day,
Allow her to see the beauty in herself and in
others.
Protect her. Keep her warm.

Oh, Woman who walks in beauty,
I am a friend now distant and silent.
I will care for you always.

When he opened his eyes Luke found a small band of children in a circle around him, staring. The lamb in his arms called out to one of them, just like a sheep at home, one who knows she belongs to one of his sister's children. To Anaba or Lillie, or Burke.

He wondered if these children named their animals, the way his nieces and nephews did.

"Tilda!" a girl called, giving him his answer.

And just like one of their churros, when placed on her feet, Tilda ran for her girl, whose light curls matched her animal's.

A boy of about eleven stepped before the others, his stance protective, his arms stiff at his sides.

"Do you understand my talk, man?" he called out.

Luke nodded.

"Are you a dirty spy?"

He shook his head. "I've had a bath."

The boy grunted out his frustration. "Are you German?"

"American." For the first time, the word did not come out of him hostile, or sounding like a lie.

The boy's frown deepened. "That was nae American words in yer singing."

The tallest girl, one on the brink of her womanhood, joined him, her eyes steady on Luke's even as she spoke to the boy.

"And what do you know of American singing, Alisdair MacArdle?" she demanded. "He's dark, maybe one of their black men. Maybe it was the jazz he was singing."

Luke smiled. "Is this the station of Ian MacArdle?" he managed a longer sentence, his own voice still sounding strange to him.

"It is," Almost Woman said.

"I am sent by Ian MacArdle's sister. To help with the shearing."

The children closed their circle in tighter.

"From the hospital at the Keep she sent you?"

"Yes."

"You're Auntie's Yank, then, from out of the Wild West of America?"

"Yes."

The Dinè Yank, he finished in his head. Born to the Salt Clan, born for the Deer People.

The tallest girl walked closer, squinted up at him, as her hands came to rest on her hips. "Do ye wear braces, man?"

As he was trying to understand what she meant, the boy Alisdair moved in, opening Luke's suit coat's lapels and peering past his open vest.

"He does, Catriona, see?" he reported, showing them all Luke's suspenders.

Almost Woman, whose given name was Catriona, smiled and nodded. "That's good. I fear your fancy cut city trousers would fall off with the stooping." She laughed a woman's laugh. "We canna have that, as fine-formed a man as you may be."

"Oh, aye, with eyes like the galloping Western horsemen in the picture shows," Tilda's Girl finished.

All the girls began giggling behind their hands then, just like the ones at home.

Women around the world enjoyed their ability to unnerve him, Luke decided.

"So," he interrupted their festival, taking advantage of the rough texture of his newly-returned voice. "Now that you are sure my trousers will stay up, will you lead me to your shears and your sheep, little grandmothers?"

They all looked to Catriona.

"If Auntie Anna says so. Best not to cross that one."

"I know," he agreed.

By the time the sun was high in the sky, Luke's every muscle ached, and he worried he'd drunk their well dry of its water. But the farmer Ian MacArdle, a slight man whose face was set in a perpetual squint against their valley's wind, grinned. "That's the lot of them, laddie," he said.

Luke had shucked the fleece off three dozen sheep, by Catriona's reckoning. He'd nicked none, and accomplished his task in forty-six strokes for the last dozen. The children laughed at their animals rolling on their bared backs in the new grass.

Sounds interrupted all the laughter. Unwelcome, mechanical sounds.

Trucks, an automobile and an ambulance appeared. They screeched to a halt before the shearing pen.

Luke opened his grandfather's watch. Spencer's men had taken three hours to hunt him down to this place, which made him wonder about the chances of the Allied war effort. Of course, Nurse MacArdle might have done some mis-directing.

Her brother joined his children as they formed a wall between Luke and his captors.

The vehicles emptied of Spencer's men, hospital officials, and Stones-in-Her-Throat in high gear.

Ian's squint deepened, making his eyes disappear. He nodded. "Sister," he acknowledged only her.

Luke touched his sleeve.

"Best stay where ye are, lad," the farmer advised, without turning. I wouldna worry yourself about the others and any displeasure they have with ye. But that one? There's no holding herself once she starts. Give her a wide berth."

The next voice was his sister's.

"Luke Kayenta, your heart is as black as the Earl of Hell's weskit!" she called out. "Traipsing off so these fine gentlemen had to spend the morning on a grand tour of the countryside to find ye!"

Her voice left its stones-in-the-brook and now rolled over thunder. "And ye'll wipe that white-toothed smile from yer face this minute! You're nae too big for a good hiding and clap on the jaw frae me!"

He opened his arms in the charged silence. "Your attention to my absence honors me, Nurse MacArdle."

She stood stock still. Her eyes weren't grey, Luke realized now, they only seemed so in his room. They reflected the colors she was near. They were the soft green of the new grass out here, at her brother's farm and sheep station.

241

"Ye found it, lad," she whispered, taking his hands in hers. "Ye found yer voice."

"Aye."

"Then ye had best let these great grey lummoxes fly ye on home, my lamb."

The End

Eileen Charbonneau is a Rita and Heart of the West award-winning author of novels and screenplays. She's been involved with theater and independent filmmaking projects, and is a storyteller of Irish and Native American tales. Eileen's multi-cultural heritage includes Shoshone relatives who were three members of the Lewis and Clark Expedition. You can reach her through her website: eileencharbonneau.googlepages.com, her blog: Manituwak.blogspot.com, on facebook as Eileen Charbonneau Author, via Twitter @EileenC1988 or by email: EileenCharbonneau@gmail.com

bookswelove.com